D1383951

Into the Interior

Into the Interior

Michelle Cliff

University of Minnesota Press

MINNEAPOLIS · LONDON

Quotations from "Stone" are from Kamau Brathwaite, *Middle Passages* (New York: New Directions Publishing, 1994); copyright 1993 by Kamau Brathwaite; reprinted courtesy of New Directions Publishing.

Published by the University of Minnesota Press
111 Third Avenue South, Suite 290
Minneapolis, MN 55401-2520
http://www.upress.umn.edu

Library of Congress Cataloging-in-Publication Data

Cliff, Michelle.
Into the interior / Michelle Cliff.
p. cm.
ISBN 978-0-8166-6979-0 (hc : acid-free paper)
ISBN 978-0-8166-6980-6 (pbk : acid-free paper)
1. Self-realization in women—Fiction. 2. Displacement (Psychology)—Fiction. 3. Bisexual women—Fiction. I. Title.
PR9265.9.C55I58 2010
813'.54—dc22

2010004553

Printed in the United States of America on acid-free paper

16 15 14 13 12 11 10 10 9 8 7 6 5 4 3 2 1

The bear-girl

The sow-girl

The wolf-child

The pig-child

The South African baboon-child

The gazelle-child

The panther-child

The snow-hen.

She has brushed her hair, perhaps for the last time, and taken off her pearl necklace, also for the last time. Now she is gazing at the candle flame, which doubles itself in the mirror. Once upon a time, that mirror was the tool of her trade; it was within the mirror that she assembled all the elements of femininity she put together for sale. But now, instead of reflecting her face, it duplicates pure flame.

She enters the blue core, the blue absence. She becomes something other than herself.

—*Angela Carter, "Impressions: The Wrightsman Magdalene"*

Contents

· I ·

{ 1 }

Points of Departure

I was born in the middle of the twentieth century and was raised in the age of Victoria, at least partly, for my family, older than the hills, older than the D'Urbervilles, cleaved to the past they had received, and the landscape, real and imagined, ordered and ruinate, kept it so. Traces of heresies overcome with green. Blindness is relatively common in the tropics. As is amputation.

Not a reliable narrator in the crew.

Great-houses with galvanized roofs and wraparound verandahs, fading from the assault of the sea, salt relentless, ghosts dressed as sea captains dancing along the corridors above the ballroom, portraits grimy with refinement, sweet to the tongue should you lick one. Everything in need of restoration.

Do not look too closely. Have you not been warned, girl?

A black maid kisses her teeth as her master tongues the gold hoop in her ear. Salt and sugar, sugar and salt—our periodic table, and rum. Trade winds bring sick, and color. Red moonlight. Boiling sea. Hurricanes pose as tempest. Crusoe loses his way, swims in Friday's footprint. Prospero dozes in Doctor's Cave, and the world turns upside down. Old into new.

On the path leading away from the great-house, the past lay in shards. Fragments of a jar promising hair growth.

China plates cut into counters for a pastime in the darkness. A brown bottleneck.

Further into the interior the impenetrable green, the fury of noise—birdsong.

Down the road from the great-house in a one-room establishment a spirit grocer, female, purveys spirituous liquors. She lights a hand-rolled cigar and squats inside the doorway out of the heat, light.

Saturday night at Tower Isle Hotel and a local band was playing "Exodus, Movement of Jah People." Cold comfort near the end of the twentieth century. Dancing across tiles scrubbed clean with kerosene that very afternoon was a man and his pearled, rouge-cheeked wife, looking for all the world like a wooden-headed dolly as her husband dipped her. "Move!"

The band was teasing the couple with the tempo. Brer 'Nancy-men signifying their contempt. Speeding up or slowing down or jerking the music around. But the pair seemed oblivious to the trickery. They danced across the tiles and landed in the garden outside by the pool, against a galvanized fence, sloganized.

> The scenery about this part is singularly romantic. Large round hills, almost hemispherical in their contour, rise out of valleys in great number . . . conical hills . . . half in glowing sunlight . . . half in deep shadow . . . unlike anything I have seen.
>
> —Philip Henry Gosse, *A Naturalist's Sojourn in Jamaica*

In 1865, the American landscape painter Frederic Edwin Church journeys into the heart of Jamaica, into the vale of

St. Thomas. He and his wife have come to the island following the deaths of their two young children. He will, in several paintings done in his studio in upstate New York from sketches he will carry home, revise the island. In one of the most famous of these paintings, completed in 1867, called *The Vale of St. Thomas, Jamaica,* originally known as *Jamaica,* he will place a monastery on a promontory overlooking the river that flows through the rainforest. There has been a passing storm; dark clouds edge the canvas.

There is no monastery where Church has painted one, but this is a man sunk in grieving. He needs to pacify the landscape, to place his beliefs, his version of humanity in it. He removes the native population, manumitted slaves, now freeholders, and abandoned planters, bereft of property.

He wants to believe, as does Alexander von Humboldt, whose *Cosmos* Church knows almost by heart, that nature is benign, that the universe is harmless. Everywhere he looks Church creates the world harmonic, sublime.

He turns from Darwin and the cruelties necessitated by natural selection, the conflict, the natural war that is everywhere as Darwin sees it, and embraces the morality of nature as von Humboldt has described it. He has lost two small children. He cannot fail to hear his wife in the night weeping.

When Church paints the monastery into *The Vale of St. Thomas, Jamaica,* he finds peace, the very thing that eludes the place, his island subject. The place of we who stone our own.[1]

Church paints the tropics sublime. He peoples his paintings with manmade and natural crosses, rainbows, auroras,

[1]Mikey Smith—foremost practitioner of "nation language"— "Stoned to death on Stony Hill"—poet supreme—speaker of the sedimented Carib tongue(s)—about whom Kamau Brathwaite wrote—"Stone"

churches. Where he once painted icebergs, monumental and white, he now paints the warm interiors of tropical places, sunlight glinting rivers, blue mountains, scarlet breast of a parrot on a palm frond.

In *The After Glow*—"The best twilight I have ever painted"; this is amusing, there is no twilight in Jamaica. The sun rushes to its rest—in the foreground, true to form, is a ruined church.

Within the Vale of St. Thomas, Jamaica, at the very time Church is there

Revolution!
—War down a Monkland

When the stone fall that morning out of the johncrow sky
it was not dark at first . . . .

& yet it was happenin happenin happenin
the fences begin to crack in i skull .
& there was a loud boodooooooooooooooooooooooongs like
guns going off . them ole time magnums .

or like a fireworks a dreadlocks was on fire .
& the gaps where the river comin down
inna the drei gully where my teeth use to be smilin .
& i tuff gong tongue that use to press against them & parade

pronunciation . now unannounce & like a black wick in i head &
dead .

When the stone fall that morning out of the johncrow sky

i could not hold it brack or black it back or block it off or limp
away or roll it from me into memory or light or rock it steady
into night . be

Which poem concludes: "i am the stone that kills me"

War down a Morant Bay
War down a Chiggerfoot
The queen never know
War oh! Heavy War oh!—
is in the air!

Firestorm passes into the Vale of St. Thomas, igniting Church's composition.

Not since the Great Slave Rebellion of Christmas 1831 has there been such a thing. Bogle and Gordon will hang for their audacity. Led to the gallows by Maroons in the service of Governor Eyre. Once the Queen catches on, she will dissolve the Jamaican Parliament, tear up the Jamaican constitution, and bestow Crown Colony status on the island, which will last one hundred years or so.

Britannia waives the rules.

And this is a point of departure.

"I saw him as clear as day."

My great-grandmother (*grand blanc,* as she's entered in the island census by a civil servant she upbraids for inattentiveness) swears to her ghost, a gallant seafarer who comes to her in the night.

My great-grandmother, half-asleep on a watery bluesilk chaise, her last good thing, where distinguished company once lounged, is speaking of courtiers and carriages and chivalric codes. The languidness of her young womanhood is transformed in old age into senility, and she is in a room in a nursing home in Kingston, a city she hates, for its sprawl, its lack of grace, and why wouldn't she?

She is of the North Coast, of Runaway Bay specifically, born on a plantation, one of the seven the family owned in its heyday, an avenue of royal palms leading to a second-story verandah whence the sea was visible just beyond a forest of coconut palms. The floor of the forest littered with the brown skulls of dried-out water coconuts.

Halls off the upstairs verandah lead to mahogany-floored rooms, high-legged four-posters, feathered head of a cacique crowning each corner, mosquito netting enshrouding each Arawak likeness. The slope of a planter's chair next to a wooden jalousie, slats turned down against the heat, light—the room becomes a dark, cool place. Silver jug of rum and volume of Carlyle or Burke sit on a rattan table.

Backstairs lead to a passageway to a kitchen where a wood fire is burning and a suckling pig is buried in the coals.

The yellow brick of the great-house began as ballast on a slaver. It is interrupted here and there by coral embedded in the walls, slashing them pink.

To encourage the exchange of breezes through the house the walls of the rooms do not reach the ceiling; there is only the illusion of privacy. Everything can be heard.

Today there is only the ruined arch of an aqueduct and skeletons of coconut trees afflicted by an airborne virus.

Tonight in the city, bands are playing, marching to the National Stadium where at midnight the Union Jack will be lowered and the black and green and yellow will be raised. Where in twenty years Bob Marley will lie in state, haloed by politricksters.

My great-grandmother is half-asleep, a stream of obscenity escapes her mouth like a sneeze, and I, aged ten, retreat.

Great-house as Flying Dutchman, caught in the wrack of the Cape of Good Hope.

The watery silk of her chaise makes the blue of my great-grandmother's eyes almost unbearable, each lighting the hook of her nose, evoking a Carib ancestor, Sephardic fugitive; who is to say?

The fires lit the skies of Spain as they unearthed the Jews.

"How the mighty are fallen!" her attendant says, regretless, eager as she is to get to the celebrations of the evening, and I, aged ten and well-schooled, picture the *vast and trunkless legs of stone* of "Ozymandias," a poem I am to recite at prize-giving under the vast bosom of the English mistress, expressed to us from Manchester.

I will be given *Ivanhoe* as a prize.

"I have things I need to tell you," my great-grandmother says to me. "I was fucked too many times."

"Lord Jesus, have mercy on she," the attendant says, then kisses her teeth.

"She walks in beauty like the night, of cloudless climes and starry skies, and all that's best of dark and light, meet in her aspect and her eyes."

Somewhere she dredges Byron.

I am ten years old then; I retreat.

In my mind's eye there are indentations in the ground. I can see the slope of coffee, the guinea grass pastures, the dirt tracks crisscrossing the place, the white marl boundaries. I can smell the sugarworks. Noisome sweetness.

Along the convolutions of my brain some of the bodies are buried.

"If I should see thee
After long years,
How should I greet thee,
In silence and tears."

Her room was naked but for a crucifix on the wall where there should have been Her Majesty. After her declaration the attendant removed even that, saying she didn't care who the old woman's people were, she had no right saying such a nasty thing in front of Jesus.

"And him 'pon de cross and everyt'ing."

One afternoon rain pounding the metallic roof of the great-house. There is no dark, no gloom like a rainy afternoon in the tropics. Rain sounding through rooms whose walls do not meet the ceiling. Humidity rising. The pages of books buckle as mildew seeps into them, foxing the pages. Romantics discolored.

A girl bent double.

On neighboring land a man's wife is dead and his daughters are living. One of the daughters gets pregnant. A landowner's attempt to secure his lineage, his name. The baby is stillborn, they say, and is buried in the family boneyard.

A girl may ask: How can so-and-so have a baby? She's not married.

A black maid giggles at the girl's confusions. "Is nuh ram goat get she? Is why de baby it bawn dead."

My great-grandmother, a girl, does not understand.

They brought another old woman into my great-grandmother's room. The two settled in side by side.

"I shall need my bloodsilk gown this evening. [Did she mean blue?] Please see that it is properly ironed."

The other old lady makes as if to set up an ironing board. Makes as if to light a brazier of coals. Makes as if to heat three flatirons beside her bed. She draws her right hand through the air, back and forth, back and forth, across her breasts, across the pretend-dress, as she breaks a sweat from the heat of the iron.

"Don't make me strike you, now. Don't make me strike you."

I am ten. I retreat.

{2}

Lying-In

The last thing in the world my mother wanted was a child. Worse: this was a daughter. Her husband, my father as it happened, made it clear. "If it's not a boy, don't bother bringing it home. Don't even think about it, you hear?"

This would pass of course. And his remarks would pass as a family joke. But the point had been made. Say no more.

The lying-in hospital was pink stucco with aquamarine trim and a terracotta-tiled roof. The grounds displayed the usual foliage: bougainvillea, hibiscus, poinciana trees, their long brown pods rattling in the breezes sent from the sea. Palm trees, yes. But none bearing fruit. No coconut palms. No risk of a concussed new mother out to enjoy a postpartum stroll. Here, within pink and blue walls, was where the bourgeoisie of the island dropped their young. Their maids and cooks and nannies, girls from country, gave birth wherever they found themselves. That was the tradition among the peasantry, common knowledge among their employers.

White-clad women walked the halls of the lying-in hospital. White-clad women with starched, winged headdresses. These were nursing nuns sent to the island from the mother house in Dublin. Nuns walking close to the stucco walls in an almost silence.

The doctor who delivered me had escaped from Austria through a pipeline that flushed him into Turkey, India, Ceylon, where he stowed away (for a price) on a British freighter servicing colonial ports of call. The doctor paid dearly for his flight. His mother and father were infirm, and he was forced to leave them behind. They insisted he go, kindly stuffing his pockets with valuables to barter his escape. He was a young man; there was no use in his remaining behind, they assured him. "Here." They gave him a new alligator skin medical bag and filled it with fine steel instruments.

The night of my birth my father was on a sailboat in Kingston Harbour at the yacht club. Impaling a local beauty, when his older sister happened on the scene, lowered herself into the well of the boat, and grabbed him by the scruff of his neck. The beauty, disengaged, fled below where she repaired herself. His sister pulled him to his feet.

"And what the hell do you think you're up to?"

After my birth they removed me to our house on the sea. My great-grandmother ran the house with an extravagant hand. Our fortunes had declined somewhat, and she sought to ignore that reality and clung to her memories of finer times. Her senility no doubt started with that. Maybe not. She remembered the seven plantations, remembered her favorite at Discovery Bay. She remembered the horses they raced and the jockeys her father imported from England, seducing them with promises of life in the tropics: women, rum, a racing scene that attracted some of the richest men in the world. Little white men arrived and were suited in the family's silks. Purple and white, with a gold bow at the front of the jockey's cap. "Riders up!"

The doctor prescribed a change of scene for my mother's melancholia, and so she and my father sailed for Cuba as soon as she was strong enough for the journey. Cuba before Castro, where you could get anything your heart desired. I was to remain behind with my great-grandmother and her staff of servants.

"What are you asking me?" My great-grandmother and my mother were colliding on the verandah seated on wicker chairs, a silver tea service between them.

"We need to hire a nanny for the child."

"I cannot be expected to support any more staff. As it is they are stealing me blind." Extravagance was not to be confused with generosity.

"We need to send to country for someone."

"What's wrong with Winona? She has been with us since the devil was a boy."

"She is too old. And she is deaf."

"Then the child's cries won't disturb her."

"What are you saying?"

"She's deaf as a post, but she will have to do."

{3}

Among the Christian Diabolists

I grew up to be someone adept at leaving.

My great-grandmother left me an evening bag made of chain mail and lined in black velvet, bald in places from age. Trapped in the folds of black was a golden guinea as bright as if minted yesterday.

Whatever became of the bag I cannot recall. I wear the coin on a chain around my neck.

My mother died the year I was twelve, subject of a raging infection following a Haitian abortion. I of course was not told this, but years later I managed to piece the story together.

My father told me she'd been on a shopping trip to Port-au-Prince, purchasing some yards of Cameroon appliqué to give her dressmaker.

"You know how stylish your mother was," my father said, explaining there was a ball in honor of the ambassador from Ghana. Africa was to be the theme of the evening.

"Black-is-beautiful, A-free-ca, have consumed this island," he went on. So Haiti, he reasoned, the closest thing to the heart of darkness, was her choice for authenticity. Home of the undead.

"She stepped off the sidewalk in front of her hotel," he went on, his eyes watering at the corners, but holding his voice firm. "She never knew what hit her."

A dray? A gaily painted bus? Truck with lettering on the side?

They flew her body back on a seaplane and she skidded into Kingston Harbour, the wake of the plane scattering the dolphins in pursuit of it.

We buried her in the family graveyard on the one remaining plantation, nearby Ocho Rios, and cast seashells at her head and feet. I experienced her death as a final absence; she who had never been a presence.

I was sent back to boarding school nearby the Vale of St. Thomas, while my father courted a former Miss Jamaica said once to have slept with Errol Flynn.

A black maid overhearing me tell this gossip to a classmate: "And which of dem haven't?"

I found a letter in my father's desk several school breaks later. I had been sent home early as punishment for sharing a spliff of ganja with one of the gardeners at the school. "Let this be a warning," the headmistress said, taking note of my recent loss and being herself merciful.

My father was playing golf at Constant Spring and I was bored, so I went into his study and began to leaf through the papers in his desk. Nothing much there until I spied a letter from the doctor who delivered me. Something about "warning you as to your wife's condition. She may be planning something foolish. I urge you would call on me to discuss this matter further."

The letter was dated two weeks before my mother's death.

Sometime later I figured out what was unsaid. In the years since, I have tried to imagine my mother's death. A stylish woman in a stylish clinic bleeding away.

. . .

I found myself in my twenties aboard an ocean liner on my way to London with vague plans of going to graduate school. I had been living in New York City, having finished college there, at a place my father referred to as "that high-priced bordello." He paid the tuition begrudgingly. As far as I knew I was the only Caribbee.

I supported myself after college doing freelance work, picture research and ghostwriting mostly. I fancied myself a citizen of the world, belonging nowhere, with fealty to no one.

My last assignment before I embarked for England was as ghost to a whistleblower who said he knew the truth about Lumumba and wanted to go public with it.

We met weekly at the Grand Central Station Oyster Bar. Over shellfish and beer he told me what he said he knew and I took notes. Details included a body being driven around and around in the trunk of a black car with diplomatic plates and an assassin who washed his hands with brown lye soap over and over—thirty-one times at one cocktail hour, by my informant's count.

According to the whistleblower, Lady MacBeth was now the station chief in Kingston, poised to trash Michael Manley. I don't know if I believed him.

Not that I would put anything past the CIA, or underestimate the insouciant megalomania of the United States. We, Jamaica, that is, had made the transition from overlord to overlord rather smoothly—with only a rustle of underthings—the odd sputter of resistance, and that mostly horizontal.

The island accommodated the ruffian of the New World as well as it had Her Majesty. Those in the upper classes (those of my great-grandmother's ilk) held themselves aloof from the ruffian, knowing they'd been taught better manners than to break bread with cowboys. Leave them to their refineries and hotels and strip mines. Let them have the white-sanded North Coast; we'll keep the dark volcanic sands of the South. She opened her legs, closed her eyes, and recalled with a sigh the days when she was fucked by royalty. Too many times.

But then Michael overstepped, making overtures to Fidel, among others.

I had come by my sense of things unexpectedly. I had shared more than hits of ganja with the workers at my boarding school. The gardener with whom I had been caught preached in a country church Sunday morning and evening. He asked me to come along, and I said yes, thank you. I wasn't particularly interested in church. But anything was better than the deadly silence of school on the Sabbath. And underneath the silence the sobs of homesick girls.

The church was whitewashed limestone and stood on a village square. A common sight in Jamaican villages. I felt conspicuous in my school uniform among the congregation in its Sunday best who at first paid me little mind.

Above the altar—what appeared to be a sewing machine table, with *Singer* cast in wrought iron between its legs—was a hand-painted sign:

Church of the Christian Diabolist
Est. Robert Wedderburn, London 1810

Hanging underneath this inscription were two machetes, crossed in an X, one blade painted red, the other black.

The gardener, also named Robert, walked up the two steps to the altar. He raised his arms and the congregation launched into the first hymn.

Oh General Jackson
Why you kill all de black men-them

What a wrongful judgment
What an awful mourning
You bring on we people-them

What I had taken for a kindness was something else. I was asked to stand up and my person became the subject of the gardener's sermon. Beginning with my school uniform and all it signified. Cross and crown over one nascent breast. Overarched with motto: *In This Sign We Prosper.*

"You seem to be somewhere else."

"Pardon?"

I was back at the oyster bar with the whistleblower who was telling me he had known Lumumba as a boy.

"How?"

He leaned forward, into his littlenecks, and whispered, "We were in the same Boy Scout troop. In Leopoldville."

"Really."

"Yes. You should be writing this down." He sucked a littleneck from its shell and chased it with a gulp of beer.

I scribbled in my notebook.

"My parents were missionaries and were sent to the Belgian Congo, as it was known then. I was born there. I often think there is a real link between being the son of missionaries and being a CIA agent."

"Saving the world on several levels, I imagine."

"Something like that. Patrice was a few years older than me. But we were in the same grade at the mission school. We camped out together once. One night on the banks of the Congo."

We seemed to be entering Huck and Jim territory.

"Don't tell me: you built a raft."

"Very amusing, but no."

"Maybe you don't want to trust me with your story."

"Why not?"

"Because I don't know if I believe you."

"So what? You're my ghost, not my judge."

"Right."

"Let me show you these photographs."

He placed two black-and-white photos on the table. One was a snapshot of two boys, one darker and taller than the other, each wearing a Boy Scout uniform with a sash bearing merit badges.

The other photo had its mate in postmortem snapshots of Steve Biko, Walter Rodney, Emmett Till.

He showed me the photos with tears in his eyes. "I have to tell the world what we did."

As if the world did not already know.

I wanted no part of this.

I stood in the church of the Christian Diabolists as they gathered around me, mocking me. Making game. Pointing. "I am not worth your merriment. I am not worth your merriment. I am not worth your merriment." I closed my eyes and repeated these words in my head, hoping they would carry me past this moment.

We were reading the War poets in school, and I had been assigned to commit Wilfred Owen to memory.

{ 4 }

Below the Waterline

I set sail.

On the crossing something quite surprising happened.

I explored the interior of a lifeboat with a fellow passenger night after night. Our cabin was cramped and shared with two others.

The lifeboat rocked us, we it, while underneath others strolled, watching out for stars, watching for ice floes in early September, which I knew as hurricane season.

I'd been lying on a bunk in a four-person cabin below the waterline. Janet Flanner's *Paris Was Yesterday* was propped on my chest, *The Female Eunuch* was on the floor. I was wearing a red T-shirt and blue jeans with a button fly. The golden guinea rested between my breasts.

The ship was still tied to the dock; the companionway outside the cabin sounded with champagne corks, laughter, people taking leave, and then the door opened and a woman about my age was standing over me.

"Do you by any chance have a needle and thread?" she asked.

Her hair was honey-colored, longish, and her eyes were black. A slender white line ran from the outside corner of her right eye to the right edge of her bottom lip.

I said that I didn't have a needle and thread, and she shrugged and sat on the bunk across from me and began to go through the duffel bag she had dragged through the door with her. Not finding what she sought she poured the contents out onto the bunk. She let out a soft "Damn" and, giving up, took off her blouse, fishing another from the pile next to her.

I tried to act as if I were interested in Janet Flanner, but her writing style became suddenly precious, and even the photographs of Paris bored me. She slid to the floor, landing on top of *The Female Eunuch.*

"Why don't you come up top with me? There's nothing quite like sailing away from New York City."

"Why not?"

"I'm Bex," she said, extending her hand. "Let's go."

Up top was festive even with a light Indian summer rain. People crowded the rails just like in the movies. Foghorns sounded up and down the Hudson. The traffic on the West Side Highway glistened in the rain.

"Come on," Bex said, taking my hand and drawing me to a space at the railing facing the piers north of us. She pointed to a white ship a few blocks away, at about 57th Street.

"That's the *Michelangelo,*" she said, and I responded with what I intended as a tone of world-weariness (intended to mask my unease, my shyness with this woman). "Yes, I know."

"My daddy died on that boat," she said, stretching out the *died* forever.

Her accent was in large part American South, exactly where I could not say, with a tinge of British now and then. My own voice was nondescript, I thought, except when tired or among those of similar ilk, when I patois-ed with the best of us, Creole to the touch, Afro-Saxon at the core. My mother tongue had been given me by Winona, who only feigned deafness; it made life easier, she said. "Den me can hignore de bitch-dem."

Bex's announcement woke me. "Oh, God," I said, "I'm so sorry."

"Oh, don't be, honey," she turned to me and smiled. "He was real, real old. Besides, he died in his element."

"Oh?"

"Daddy was a sculptor. He wasn't a very good one but he had a lot of money, so that was neither here nor there. We were on our way back from Carrara. Daddy wanted to get some marble from where Michelangelo got his. And he did. He brought the whole family. Me; my stepmothers—he called them the three disgraces—they all lived together as if we were Mormon or something; my sister, a Buddhist nun—no, I am not putting you on—high, in every sense, in the Himalayas like in *Black Narcissus*; and my brother, back from a tour of duty in Vietnam, not quite there, he lived in black silk pajamas."

She paused. "He, my brother, kept saying he wanted to go and live in the Great Dismal Swamp. Daddy brought him along to try and convince him otherwise. Well, honey, he's there now, eating freeze-dried food and searching the swamp for booby traps."

"What happened to your father?"

"Oh, yeah. There was this big storm outside of Naples. Daddy was below, in the hold, watching over his big block of marble. Standing guard over it like it was King Kong. With all the rocking and rolling in the storm the marble broke loose. Boom! That was that."

"Jesus." But I could not help laughing; nor could she.

"At least it was quick. We signed some papers absolving the shipping company, and they put him on ice. Had to deep-six a ton of gelato to make room, which did not exactly endear us to the other passengers. Who could blame them? The three disgraces took turns standing vigil in front of the freezer. When we landed we got through customs real fast because we had this dead body—I mean we could have brought anything in. We buried him back home in Maryland and put the block of marble there to mark the spot. It seemed appropriate."

We slid from the berth and made our way downriver. The light rain was misting into fog. I was watching the rain and the harbor as we entered it from the river. As if the scene were painted. People used to come to New York City for the air and the light. Even with the rain and fog the light was extraordinary. We passed under the bridge. Behind us the islands stood discrete.

Ambrose Light passed by and the bells onboard rang, signaling lunch. Behind us and in front of us was nothing but ocean. The same flat line encircled us. At that moment my whereabouts were unknown, which comforted me.

"Shall we?"

Below was the dining room. Low-ceilinged, dimly lit, with wildly floral wallpaper, gilt chairs, and enormous portions of ocean liner food.

Our waiter is identified by his nametag as from Goa. He tells us halfway into the voyage that he is indentured for seven years, working off a family debt. At first he is shamefaced; later, sensing outrage, conspiratorial.

The best he can do is set off a few false alarms, routing passengers out of their cabins and onto the decks, causing inconvenience.

"It is of no use," he says. "I am stuck."

. . .

"Maybe I'll go to graduate school," I say to Bex.

"In what?"

"History?"

"You don't sound very enthusiastic."

"I'm not. I have to do something."

"I'm going back to be with my husband."

This surprises me, and I show it.

"Yes, my dear, I'm married." She pauses, smiles. "To the man who would be queen. Makes travel easier; you know, crossing frontiers. He's a sweetie, by the way."

We are sitting in one of the ship's bars, watching the sun go down. The red sky is about to suffuse the flat line. Soon the sky will contain Church's *After Glow.*

Bex holds her Gibson aloft as if paying tribute.

Actually she's counting the onions in her drink.

"If the bartender were righteous, he'd have put only two onions in this drink. Know why?"

"No."

"Take a wild guess."

Her right hand is under the table, resting lightly on the inside of my left thigh.

"I've no idea."

"They're for the nipples of the Gibson Girl, darlin'."

But the bartender, unknowing, has filled the glass to the brim with gin and vermouth and five pearl onions.

"She might as well be a sow, honey."

Who do you think is coming to town you better guess who

Bex doesn't miss a beat.

huggable loveable Emily Brown, Miss Brown to you

A dream on shipboard: two people (faceless) and I are in a stark white room with white sand on the floor. The light in the room is blinding.

One of them says, "We've got a sandwish for you made from the Mistral."

In the dream the word is *sandwish.* Meaning?

The sandwich bulges at the sides as the Mistral tries to escape.

Gabriela Mistral?

The ship is passing through a gale. There is no one on deck but the two of us. Bex is playing the flute. The sheet music is long gone, having been whipped away in the wind. The notes pass through us and are taken by the gale.

We are suspended above the promenade deck, our motion matching the motion of the ship. I am lying at the bottom of the lifeboat in the darkness, her tongue is working me. I feel myself open as the flood rises. Bits of conversation drift up. Below passengers are discussing tomorrow's arrival at Southampton. There will be one last chance at the gaming tables tonight before the end of this floating world in the morning. Words overlap. We pay them little attention.

Now we are face to face. I can taste myself on her tongue. Salt. Conch.

I draw my finger along the scar on her face.

She takes it away. "That's a long story, darlin', and extremely unpleasant. Take my word for it."

"Will we ever see each other again?"

"You tell me."

"You."

She went into a bar one night just outside Charlottesville. She ordered a drink and then went into the ladies' room. Inside, in front of the mirrors, were some sorority sisters she recognized from the university. "Pardon me if this reeks of cliché."

"One of them came over to me as soon as I came through the door. She asked me if it was true what people said about me. I asked her what she meant, although of course I knew, I was stalling for time. And she said in her best cunt-huntry voice, 'That you're a fucking queer.' I didn't say anything, I just turned to leave, hoping against hope they wouldn't pursue me. I knew well the danger of a gauntlet of girls.

"Then. They were on me. Just like that. I was on the floor on my back and one of them was choking me. I recall smelling quinine and gin and Winstons. No one spoke. There was not one fucking sound. Then two of them held me down while my original accuser applied a razor blade to my face, as cool as if she were applying eyeliner, and just as good at it. I felt that awful chill when something sharp, you know, paper, a shard of glass, cuts you and it takes time for the blood to come. I had closed my eyes. Then I felt a warmth and wetness. I tasted it as it ran into my mouth. I don't think I said anything, I don't remember. In my memory the entire thing plays out in silence.

"Then I felt the blade being drawn across my throat. Not deep enough to kill me, but deep enough—like Mercutio.

"Here comes the comical part. After they left me—and they left without a word—I searched in my handbag for a quarter, all the while praying the Kotex dispenser wouldn't be empty. Jesus, I was a mess. I just wanted to get out of there with a minimum of notice. There was one pad in the dispenser. I held it to the side of my face while the blood from my throat ran between my breasts, like perspiration. Not a soul in the bar took notice of me, and I realized that during the entire business no one had come into the ladies' room. I mean, this was Friday night at a college hangout.

"I drove myself to the hospital in the black part of town and made up a story about having a drunken boyfriend. One too many at a frat party and boom!"

"Why the black hospital?" which even as I asked it sounded strange.

"It felt safe. Like the flip side of Bessie Smith."

That remark jarred me. Layered as it was in a history, a skein of relationships I could not pretend to understand.

"They patched me up. Sent me on my way. I got in my car and drove to a cabin my family had and stayed there for a while."

The voices below were gone. There was no sound but the noise of the ship's engine and the waves licking at the waterline.

I ran my finger along the white line of her scar. She did not take it away.

Her husband met the ship at Southampton. He was as she described. Flamboyant and sweet.

"You two certainly look well rested," he greeted us.

"That we are," Bex said, and he kissed her on each cheek.

"Will you drive up to London with us?" he asked.

"I don't think so, but thanks."

"Are you sure?"

"Yes."

I kissed her good-bye and went to look for the train.

{5}

Marooned

I hid away in an institute of advanced learning whose specialty is the visual arts, awash in nudes and ambiguity.

"We study the dreams of the past," the director tells me. I have walked in off the street and gained an audience.

Everything is red and gold and lapis. So comforting, all this color, evidence of grandeur. So much easier on the eyes than a black-and-white photograph of Patrice Lumumba rotting in a fetal position in the trunk of a black sedan.

I am introduced around to my new colleagues.

The most brilliant student at the institute is Jennifer. Her mind seems to frighten her. So much so she is addicted to television. She watches *Coronation Street* religiously and can be heard in the halls of the institute, among the incunabula, humming the saxophone line from the theme song.

I don't take sex as seriously as I suppose I should. Perhaps a resonance of my motherless state, or nativity in that part of the world where sex is a sport—although within strict guidelines. Let's put it this way: if my fellow islanders caught me in the lifeboat with Bex, they'd probably incise me the way they incise pubescent girls in the tribal homeland. Chilling.

A Friday night in a ladies' room in an American college town would be as nothing.

But I'm here, and no one knows where I am.

I am drawn in Jennifer's direction even though I've moved in with an African (white) photographer (male) I met one afternoon in the National Gallery cafeteria. That's right, more snaps of the dark continent are in store. But more about that later.

I soon enough realize that anything physical with Jennifer will not be possible. She craves normalcy, and who could blame her?

She tells me she grew up in a house with glass curtains where no one could see in.

To the uninformed everything about her seems golden, but that is a common misperception.

We study beauty here and are not encouraged to look behind the canvas, stick our fingers into the wet fresco.

Jennifer and I go out together one evening. I have tickets for *Hedda Gabler.* I collect Hedda Gablers the way other people might collect Uncle Vanyas or Hamlets. I am drawn to the hollow at the center of the play. In the cold of that place, her place in it, inside and out, she is white-hot. White-hot and the heat has nowhere to escape. And so she is consumed.

The most astonishing Hedda I ever witnessed was an amateur production in St. Ann's Bay, a market town on the North Coast. Close by the ruined arch of an aqueduct. Out of doors, under the watch of a half-moon, with trade winds rustling the lime trees behind us, releasing their scent into the night. Next door to this place was a chicken coop, with several barefoot children perched on its zinc roof, attending the play.

Hedda was a dark-skinned woman in a lime green dress, her feet in thonged sandals, her toenails painted a dark red. The other cast members were light-skinned, with the familiar wave of tropical hair, and dressed to approximate Ibsen's descriptions. Judge Brack wore a white linen suit. Tesman, a sea island cotton shirt and khaki trousers. Ejlert Lovborg, a loose-fitting silk shirt awash with pirates, Spanish galleons, pieces of eight.

All were members of a little theater group from the local Anglican church. They were directed by the vicar's wife, who'd also done amateur theatricals at her last colonial outpost in Kuala Lumpur.

In life Hedda was a schoolteacher. Judge Brack a pharmacist. Lovborg worked in the post office. Tesman was a barman at the Sans Souci. Bertha a politician's wife. And Aunt Julie, making her entrance in a straw hat with akee and breadfruit and mango spun in wildly colored raffia, kept one of those country shops with magazines and romance comics pinned to a clothesline over the counter, shelves of condensed milk and Nescafé and Ovaltine, and a large barrel of dried cod, ancient victual, in the front of the shop.

Provincialism was something each well knew. A national characteristic.

Sweat beads gather in Hedda's cleavage as the moment of truth approaches when she will be ensnared by Judge Brack.

She paces, her sandals slapping across the stage.

She exits behind closed curtains—in this production, a rattan screen.

"Don't flatter yourself, Judge Brack. Now you are cock of the walk!"

She cannot resist kissing her teeth.

At which the vicar's wife releases a small sigh.

There is a rooster on the zinc roof. He crows the moment Hedda speaks her curtain line, and a feather lifted by a trade wind wafts onto the settee where she prepares to blow out her brains.

The children howl from their perch.

Hedda rises from her deathbed and points one of General Gabler's pistols in their direction.

"Is who you mek game at, eh?"

The vicar's wife bows her head.

After the play—Glenda Jackson this time, without incident—Jennifer and I go into a pub in Soho for a drink. She begins to tell me the story of her childhood, which she remembers, she says, as if through a glass curtain.

"We all do," I say, not having a clue, thinking amnesia a blessing.

"No, listen," she says.

She tells of a house with a child at dead center. A stone cottage with French doors that open on a garden of antique roses, set in the village where Guenevere took refuge on her flight to France in a church with a Norman tower.

"A small place filled with shadows. You could catch the shade of Guenevere hidden, kneeling in the dark, afraid."

The child was her sister.

"My mother was determined."

That the child speak one word, one single word. This child who lolls, head back, eyes unfocused.

"As if she emerged from the forest," Jennifer says, "from an infant asylum. Appeared in a German village from nowhere, she speaks only incoherent noise.

"No one can imagine what—if—she sees. Shapes? Colors? With no language to describe them, what meaning could they hold for her? She must be so terrifyingly lonely."

If she knows what loneliness is, I think, then say: "Yes; she must be."

"Perhaps she will fall in love someday," her mother says.

"Don't be absurd, my dear," her husband, a GP, says. He

pours his wife a gin and tonic, lights her Benson & Hedges. Like most women, he thinks, she hasn't got a clue.

"I don't see why not," she insists, "with our help."

"What was wrong with her?"

"You mean *is*. She's very much alive."

"What, then?"

"Born that way; that's all."

"How much younger than you?"

I am an only-born, semi-orphan castaway, shooting in the dark.

"She's the older one, actually."

"Really?"

"Yes. By five years. I must say it took nerve for them to try again. Although I suspect I'm insurance—you know, to take her on once they're dead."

"I can't imagine . . ." A fate worse than death to my mind, but I keep silence.

"She's been a centripetal force, drawing us in, encircling her—whether we want it or not. My mother has turned her into someone she believes she needs, not to say deserves. Rather like having a perpetual infant, I imagine."

Still I can't say anything. What does she want me to say? Does she seek comfort? Outrage?

"God, that house. If you could have seen it; no, heard it. Opera blasting, my father trying to drown out Valerie, her grunts and squeals, her rattling the bars of the playpen where she was kept, bang in the center of the drawing room. The endless conversations about possibilities. Shall we try Berlin this year? Zurich? They're making remarkable strides. On and on.

"It's the worst thing, you know."

"Having a sister like—"

"No," she interrupted, "not knowing the meaning of the sound someone makes."

Several weeks later Jennifer was informed she'd been given a grant to Milan.

"How was it?"

"God, I had the most marvelous time."

"Tell me."

"They let me turn the pages of the Codex Atlantico. They left me alone with it. Imagine. That, plus several amazing nights with a gorgeous waiter. He spoke not a word of English, or pretended not to. And I pretended not to know any Italian. It was perfect."

I envied Jennifer her enthusiasm, for Leonardo, that is. I had yet to choose a subject for study.

Morag was doing her dissertation on the appearance of the anticlockwise spiral in Michelangelo's *Last Judgment,* a mess of a painting—as any event should be no doubt—with its contorted Christ, his hands in the pose of a flamenco dancer. Bringing to mind Ava Gardner in *The Barefoot Contessa.*

I didn't understand why anyone would try to find one clean line through something so busy, so rife with panic. Superman Christ looming over the rest of us, scared past death.

Morag had been raised in the Hebrides in the tradition of John Knox and said she'd been drawn to the final judgment as a matter of course.

Morag was married to Roland, another Scot. Roland was away visiting his father, a publican in Inverness. Michael, the man I was living with, was away on assignment in Johannesburg. Soweto was under way.

I phoned one afternoon and invited Morag over.

Michael's apartment was across from the building with the blue plaque commemorating William Butler Yeats, "where Sylvia Plath forgot to check the pilot light," Michael said. "Sorry but I reserve no patience for suicides. Life is too fucking precious."

Michael had decorated the flat as an Anglo-African might. Bits of skin and ivory, a couple of bucolic scenes of life at the waterhole. A Kongo funerary jar usually held his cameras: three Nikons, one Rolleiflex. The fridge was crammed with film and beer. The sepia portrait of a man and a woman—unsmiling, in the familiar pose of their time: woman seated, hands folded in her lap, man standing behind her, one hand folded over her right shoulder—hung in the entryway. At the foot of the double bed where we slept was a beaten-up old trunk, carried into the interior by Michael's great-grandfather (the man in the studio portrait) on an expedition to cut the Cape to Cairo Railroad.

An uncut diamond sat on the bedside table, another piece of the legacy. About the size of a marble, bits of dirt stuck in its crevices.

Morag came over and we decided to stroll through the Saturday market in Camden Town. We browsed the stalls, settling in among some Battersea boxes, standing in unusual autumn sunlight side by side among other people's mementos. Brighton Pavilion. Golliwog. Gurkha. Their surfaces crazed by time.

"Can you not hear me?"

Silence. Then static.

"I'm trying to tell you . . . schoolchildren . . . their uniforms . . . stones in their fists . . . pockets."

He was calling from Johannesburg.

". . . unbearably moving . . ."

Finally the connection came clear.

"I've been reading about it in the papers."

"Take to the third power whatever it is they say."

"Tell me something?"

"What?"

"Would you pick up stones and put down your camera?"

"That's terribly tired."

"I know. When will you be back?"

"Not sure. I'll let you know."

"Take care," I said.

"Bye," he returned.

Morag and I buy a picnic and find a spot on Hampstead Heath, high up where I imagine gallows once stood and miscreants swayed, transmogrified into crows, clacking over the greensward.

Today the sky is perfectly clear. No blackbirds in sight.

Not a sign of the last judgment.

Some things happen when you least expect them. We pass a bottle of wine between us and soon we are lying side by side on a blanket Michael bought at the side of the road in Accra. On it, he tells me, so the old woman who sold it to him said, appliquéd lions and leopards stand in for kings, heroes.

He so loves the place he comes from. I admire him for that.

"Do you mind if I kiss you?" Morag asks, her Calvinist pallor giving way to high color, getting higher.

"Why?" I ask.

"I thought it might be fun," she says. "There's nobody about; our boys are away."

Has she made a presumption of unbridled sensuality as some do when they contemplate my tropical aspect? One

American boy, holding me too close, his body a monument to sweat, actually said, "Gee, I guess that means you can get into all those neat positions." Spoken with the logic of Cuvier contemplating the Venus Hottentot.

I turn my face to hers. I can see the beginnings of the spidery capillary lines pale skin is prone to.

Suddenly, glancing over my shoulder, she screams.

"What?"

"Listen, girl," she burrs.

I listen. The sound is unmistakable. At least for those of us who endured triple features in the open air of the Rialto on the Windward Road. *The Black Shield of Falworth.* Houseboys on their evening off exhorting Tony C., as they call him. And Errol Flynn, *Captain Blood,* walks among us. He was an honored guest at my christening and absconded with one of the godmothers from the garden party afterward. "Quite the cocksman, him." Backstairs wisdom. "Tasmanian Devil fe true."

But that's neither here nor there.

Swords are clanking in the near distance.

"The pellet with the poison's in the flagon with the dragon, the vessel with the pestle has the brew that is true. No, wait!"

"Shush," Morag cuts off my Court Jester.

She is not amused. In her line of vision men in armor are about to descend on us. Calvinism is not a boon to the imagination, not to mention irony.

I switch texts:

"The Assyrian came down like a wolf on the fold,
And his cohorts were gleaming in purple and gold:
And the sheen of their spears were like stars on the sea,
When the blue wave rolls nightly on deep Galilee."

"Acch," Morag sighs, reprimanding me. In thrall to tribal memory perhaps, her pallor returns. Her venture into the Malabar Caves over.

And I, of sound colonial patterning—"Pay attention, girls. Who is the poet?" "Lord Byron, Miss," in unison. "And the poem?" "The Destruction of Sennacherib, Miss." Destroyer of Babylon—say Amen: "And the might of the Gentile, unsmote by the sword / Hath melted like snow in the glance of the Lord!"

Finally, clarity: "Cut! Print!"

The knights relax.

A tea lady brings tea.

In my mind's eye there is a glass divider. On the other side of this clear wall two women are shouting. Their arms move wildly. Their mouths gape. I can hear nothing but the sound of the train.

I think I recognize one of these women. I cannot tell you her name, even now.

I am stuck behind this glass in a car on the Underground watching alternative theater. I cannot take my eyes off the two women, one of whom I barely know. I am wearing dark glasses. She is kicking at the Underground seats. I do not remember what time of day it is, but they are the only two people in the car.

Her family keeps a box at Covent Garden. Several weeks ago she took me to the ballet. She asked me out of the blue, after a lecture by Anthony Blunt, Surveyor of the Queen's Pictures, Fourth Man, who spoke to us on French architecture: the Parisian townhouse in particular. The ballet was John Cranko's *Poème de l'Exstase.*

I am afraid she will see me through the glass.

After the ballet we have supper in a restaurant near the theater. Across the street the blue plaque says this is the house in which De Quincey wrote his *Confessions.*

The Underground stops. She finally looks through the glass divider. I look down. She gets off the train. The other woman is seated, is staring out the automatic door. As the doors glide shut she shouts something.

"Go on then!"

I hear that.

"See if I care!"

That was a Friday afternoon.

On Monday morning a landlady in Hammersmith uses her key to enter her tenant's flat. She'll tell the police she had a sense something was amiss. That her tenant was a strange girl whom another girl visited at all hours.

She finds the young woman in the bath, in water tinted pink. The towel warmer has been turned on—Whatever for? the landlady wonders, wanting to look anywhere but at the girl in the bath—and the bars of the space heater glow red in a corner by the toilet. Pink water, red bars. A note has been propped between the mirror and the basin. The mirror sweats from the humidity in the room. The note curls. "To those who may find me, please forgive me."

The landlady, shaking her head, leaves the room and calls the police. While she waits she searches the flat for any sign of next of kin. Not a sign. No photos. No letters but for a few on the desk, all in the same hand, with expressions that disgust the landlady. She wonders why people leave such a mess; what possesses them?

"How was the ballet?" Michael asks me, looking up from one of his photography books.

"Quite interesting."

He balances two pictures in his lap, one on each thigh. A marketplace with a graffitied wall:

The child is not dead

Die kind is nie dood

his mother who shouts Afrika! shouts the breath of freedom and the veld

in the locations of the cordoned heart

SUBVERSION

OR

THEIR VERSION

why join the army when you can get stoned at home?

The child

VIVA!

lies with a bullet through his head

The child is the shadow of the soldiers

The child who has become a man

The sky is falling on your head PW

treks through the whole of Africa

travels through the whole world

Without a pass

WELCOME TO THE LAST SUPPER[1]

---

[1]The lines of poetry on the graffitied wall are from a poem by Ingrid Jonker, "The Child Who Was Shot Dead by Soldiers at Nyanga." Jonker (1933–1965) was the daughter of Abraham Jonker and Beatrice Cilliers. After her parents' divorce she and her sisters were raised in poverty in Cape Town, moving from room to room as her mother sought work. Her father went on to become a member of the South African parliament, and chair of a committee to enforce a law imposing censorship on printed work and entertainments. In this Jonker publicly disagreed with her father.

Her first collection of poetry, *Rook en Oker* (Smoke and Ochre), was against "Scenes drawn on the back of a soldier's tunic. Amazing, isn't it?" was Michael's answer to my "What on earth is that?"

The tunic, the caption said, dated from about 1900. Black ink on khaki. Artist unknown. A couple of scenes on horseback. One of a house—a farmhouse from the looks of it—aflame. A cannon. A ship. A gathering of native huts. And everywhere, soldiers.

"Rumor has it Cranko is a Cape Coloured."

"Really?"

"I know that sort of thing interests you."

"You'd never guess from Fonteyn's performance."

We laugh; he closes the book. "What a place," he says and gets up to pour us each a glass of wine.

The only question in the universe is "What are you going through?" I think Simone Weil said that, but I cannot remember the citation.

When the news of the suicide gets around the institute, I don't take it back to the apartment. And until now I never tell anyone what I saw through the glass divider.

I take the Underground to Hammersmith and walk past the house where it happened. I find the landlady sweeping the steps. I tell her I knew her tenant, that we were studying in the same place, and she asks to tell me her story. We sit in her kitchen and drink tea.

"The police finally located the mother and father, but

---

received with acclaim among the politically astute but was coolly received by the majority of South African (read: white) readers. Ingrid Jonker died when she walked into the Atlantic Ocean (that boneyard of boneyards) at Green Point in Cape Town. A posthumous selection of her poetry titled *Kantelson* (Setting Sun) was published in 1965.

they wouldn't come down, would they, to claim the body on account of the way she died, they said. But you can't tell me it wasn't part because of her strangeness, you know what I mean, I'm sure, as if they didn't share in the blame. What a way to be."

Michael and I have made love that morning; I find that comforting. I stand back. At a distance.

At dinner the evening of the ballet our conversation was contained. We talked about the ballet for the most part. I tell her I enjoyed it and thank her for inviting me. The last time I could only get a partially restricted view, which meant that Nureyev danced a now-you-see-him-now-you-don't *Agon.*

We spoke about the institute, which I'd yet to take seriously. I don't remember if she said what she'd chosen to write about.

"Are you really Jamaican?"

"Yes," I tell her.

"You don't seem at all like our Jamaicans."

I look past her at the whitewashed wall. There are posters advertising opera. Janet Baker as Orpheus. Callas in *Tosca.* TeKanawa as Desdemona.

"Why are you smiling?" she asks me.

"Nothing."

Jennifer's mother turns up one afternoon at the institute. Some of us are in the common room, smoking. Tied to her wrist is her firstborn. The mother wears a tweed skirt, twinset, and pearls, looks right out of *Country Life,* the perfect apparel for a country doctor's wife, but for the accessory of her child, a woman in her twenties, slightly hunched.

The mother asks after Jennifer's whereabouts, and I tell her Jennifer is probably at her desk in the stacks. I am making every effort not to look at Valerie, who is nonstop motion, nonstop sound. Sometimes her voice is pitched low, like a growl, sometimes high, like a baby bird. These are my perceptions; I have no idea what she signifies.

The pair is on the run, Jennifer tells me later.

There has been an incident in the village where they live. Valerie escaped from her room and was seen wandering in the road, her hands stroking herself between her legs. A crowd of schoolchildren were following her, laughing. Her noise becomes loud, louder, and carries into the doctor's practice. His wife, asleep in an upstairs room, is none the wiser. He has given her something to make her sleep; she's been run ragged lately. The doctor leaves his practice and uses his authority to disperse the schoolchildren, who are whistling, surrounding his daughter, chanting for Valerie to take off her clothes. Her noise is terrible; she is hideous, her father thinks.

The schoolchildren retreat and the doctor wraps a sheet around his daughter to contain her and half-drags, half-carries her back home.

He calls a surgeon.

When his wife finds out what he intends, she takes Valerie by the hand and strings a length of grosgrain between them. She leaves the house with this daughter who's been kept out of sight, until now, and takes the train to London to ask Jennifer's help.

"She thought she was safe there," Jennifer says, "that she could keep her safe."

"What did she want from you?"

"She wanted me to persuade my father not to go ahead with his decision."

"Did you?

"I spoke to him but he said it was out of the question."

"You tried at least."

"She had this pathetic plan that she and Valerie would go underground. But of course she doesn't have her own money, and no possible way of making a living. I doubt she's ever written a check. This has been her life's work. To my surprise she asked me to come with them. I said no. I suppose I was to be the man. I said no."

"What will happen now?"

"They've gone back. My father will have his way. This is something he's probably always wanted. And that doesn't make him a dreadful person, you know."

"No; I don't think it does."

"It's us who create the monsters, not men," Jennifer says. "They only clean up after us."

Imogen and Bart are language tutors at the institute. Imogen teaches French and is translating Descartes's dreams. Bart teaches Latin and Italian. He is presently involved with Boccaccio's *Genealogy of the Gods.* He had big plans: he'd fly to Rome and meet with Pasolini and convince the director to make a companion piece to the *Decameron.*

Bart longed to make a film in Latin.

But then the director was murdered by a street hustler (or government agent, as Bart preferred, thinking the other ignominious) and that was the end of that.

Imogen and Bart might have been twins. Same black hair, fair skin, blue eyes. Same indeterminate slenderness. Draped in M&S sweaters and worn corduroy slacks. Same background: grammar school in the Midlands, then Cambridge.

They kept a sailboat in Essex.

I went along with them once.

On land they were as brother and sister.

On shipboard Bart beat his wife.

They weighed anchor on their thirty-foot sailboat and moored near Colchester, taking the Colne estuary toward the sea.

Neither came from money, and it was never explained whence the money for the boat came. Certainly not from their stipends as language tutors.

Smuggling—guns, drugs, porn?

They filled the galley with tinned meat and baked beans and a coffee and chicory mixture called Camp, an unctuous black liquid whose logo was a pith-helmeted colonial being served tent-side by a red-sashed native wearing a turban. The servant was saying something in small print on the label.

The stove in the tiny galley was fueled by spirits, and I, unaccustomed to seasickness (thanks to Bex), retched from the fumes and threw up into some corned beef hash I'd been assigned to heat up, for which poor Imogen caught hell.

"Round the rugged rock, the ragged rascal ran."

That came to mind, another remnant of boarding school, as Bart pursued Imogen round and round the deck. To escape feelings that I should be doing something, somehow stopping this, I went below. This had nothing to do with me, I told myself. I poked around the cabin while their feet pounded above my head. A crate was stowed under one of the bunks. Through the slats on top I could glimpse bits and pieces of naked individuals, captioned in a language that appeared Scandinavian. Porn on the North Sea? The thumping had stopped; there was silence now but for the slap of water against the boat.

The next morning Bart decided to catch a fish for breakfast, but all he managed was a soldier crab wrapped in toilet paper.

He hit Imogen.

"Bloody scavenger," he said.

Each of us slept cocooned in a sleeping bag. Each of us on a shelf belowdecks as the water cradled us.

Before he beat her, Bart put on his sailing cap and told Imogen her breasts in her padded bra were like two peas in two colanders.

He pounded her into the finely waxed teak of the deck as the boat pitched and rolled in the sea's arm. One of her contact lenses popped out and lodged irretrievably between the planks. Imogen said nothing and continued the trip one-eyed. When I finally broke my silence, that awful pretense that nothing unusual was going on, she only shook her head.

"If you say anything it will only make him worse. It only helps if you pretend not to notice."

"That is becoming more and more difficult. Isn't there anything?"

"You could read to me from Descartes."

"It's two against one." I was suddenly Mr. Christian instigating mutiny.

"Don't be bizarre."

"Have you not thought of leaving?"

"Oh, no, no, no; I can't do that. You couldn't possibly understand."

"I guess not," I said, and that was that.

I wondered why I had been invited along. If not witness, then audience.

"Perhaps we should seek out the secret waters," Bart said to me while Imogen was occupied elsewhere.

I felt a primitive urge to do him damage. I saw him facedown in rough waters, among medieval visions of sea monsters, flat earth, nightmare. He should have no mercy.

I held my tongue.

On the last day—thank God it had come—as we motored back to the berth, Bart held his closed fist over Imogen's open palm. She flinched. He unclenched his hand and her contact lens dropped into her palm. She grasped it, licked it, and slid it back into her eye.

"A bit scratched no doubt, a bit the worse for wear," Bart said.

"Thank you, my love," she said.

Michael and I met an elephant man, a real-life collector of elephants. He was treating us to pheasant and claret on New Bond Street and telling us all about the vanishing herds in Kenya.

"Rather like your buffalo," he said to me.

I didn't bother to correct him. Each country had its disappearing, disappeared. What was the difference?

He spoke of one old bull who'd evaded the poachers for years. The elephant man, he preferred that title to white hunter, was very attached to him. He wanted Michael to bring his camera, "and her too, if you like," indicating me. The idea was to run a photospread of old Ahmed in *Life* or *National Geographic,* to draw attention to "the plight of the wild," as he put it, specifically the African elephant.

Michael told him he was flattered but that he had commitments elsewhere in Africa.

"The human element, I suppose."

"Apartheid."

"That's the thing about Africa," the elephant man said,

"one must choose. All I can tell you is that it's a bloody state of emergency right now, thanks to the bloody poachers. And the bloody corrupt governments. Black power be damned."

With that he signaled the waiter for the check.

"I need to get back," Michael told me as we walked toward the Tube.

"I know you do."

"Will you be all right here?"

"Me? Why wouldn't I be?"

"Money, whatever."

"I'll be fine, not to worry."

"I'll leave you names, freelance connections."

"Great, thanks."

"I may decide to stay."

"I thought as much."

"Our friend back there, a bit of a throwback. Resents the poachers because they have taken the sport away."

"Do you think so?"

"Believe me, I know the type. All that sentimental crap about old Ahmed. The one who's earned the great white's respect by evading his own slaughter."

"When I was small I was taken into a hotel kitchen on the North Coast. There I was introduced to a man who had cooked for us when I was a baby. I was told upon leaving by the uncle who brought me that 'Sonny,' as he was called, would never be happy in his new situation. That he 'wasn't ready for independence.' The man was working in a hotel kitchen, for God's sake."

"Why don't you fly out with me?"

"And do what?"

"See it for yourself. You might become inspired."

"I'll think about it."

We left it at that.

I'd heard rumors about the study of art history and the dangers it posed to one's sexuality.

Why art historians should be queerer than other historians intrigued me. (Why it mattered was another question.) Although they did seem to have more fun. And it was hard to envision a historian of the American presidency with enough imagination to be deviant.

Certainly some of the great *kunstgeschichtsschreibern* (particularly the Viennese) were terrifically straight. No doubt the condition varied from period to period, ethos to ethos. If one's field were Gothic architecture, edifices built by God-terrorized peasants, the wages of sin carved into the left-hand door, the devil's gateway, the likelihood of being gay might diminish, when the cathedral of study would ordain burning the student at the stake, rose windows dancing in the firelight.

But, keeping to the religious motif, were one to study the Sistine ceiling, the coupling of God and oh-so-languid Adam—perhaps connecting the portrait to sonnets Michelangelo wrote Tommasso Cavallieri—well then, Ninth Circle here I come.

Not to mention the feather of Goliath's helmet curling up the inner thigh of Donatello's David; first freestanding nude since antiquity, by the way.

I remember a Finnish scholar who visited the institute and gave a three-hour lecture on Plato's Academy, introducing the fact—if fact it was—that the inscription over the door read None Enters Here Unless He Is a Geometer and proceeded to sing of a geometer I'd never heard of, while at the same time suggesting Plato's reputation was a bit inflated, which took guts since Neoplatonism was practically speaking the institute's official religion.

His parting shot was unforgettable, delivered in his singsong accent enhanced by prelecture whiskey: So-and-so (the geometer, whose name escapes me) was absolutely heterosexual, which goes to prove there was a rose amidst all those pansies.

There it was, the source of his fervor.

Cleverness, I suppose it neither hurt nor helped.

There was also a visit from a famous polymath (actor, comedian, scholar, composer, stage director, etc.) who gave a talk on the discovery of ectoplasm, which he said coincided with a "particularly nasty wave of masturbation across Europe." Young men were squandering their birthright, he explained. The ghostly (and to his mind spermatic) emanation represented not the past, dead souls, but the escaping future.

One might draw a line, the polymath said, from the clouds of sperm to the trials of Oscar Wilde to the slaughter of World War I, all he insisted leading to the diminishment of the ruling class.

I remember a quite fierce argument between two elderly scholars about whether actors in mystery plays stood on hollow jars to magnify their voices.

As good a pastime as any, I suppose. The danger only lay in taking it too seriously.

I'd been invited to an Easter egg hunt at the home of a friend in Blackheath.

Recently divorced, she been left with the house, two children, and a big-bosomed, flaking plaster nude.

Her husband, author of a study of Isabella d'Este as connoisseur, proved himself not much of either, husband or connoisseur, and split with the German au pair, a girl with severe overbite and an advanced case of crabs.

"And I found out *after* she'd run her fucking jeans with the family wash."

Annie was left to do her best.

The house was a mess. Falling apart, with a madly overgrown garden and a view of an unmarked graveyard for "Women Who Have Come to Grief," itself rampant with growth, no doubt helped along by the decomposing grief-stricken, the potash from their bones making the yew trees flourish. I gazed at the legend over the entrance to the graveyard and connected these women in my head with the Battersea boxes, and in my mind's eye furnished small rooms with a single bed, table, chair, washbasin, and a couple of souvenirs of a life to herself. I was remembering the maid's rooms I used to haunt as a child, out back where I thought life was, making myself a nuisance.

"How am I going to get any work done, if you keep bothering me so?"

Would I have considered my great-grandmother, my mother, among the women who had come to grief? That did not occur to me.

In the evening in the graveyard owls gathered and huge ravens swept in dark, feathery clouds across the heath. Annie told me at dusk one evening she'd seen a circle of blackbirds, wings folded, silent, chanting over the dead body of another of them.

"As if they were in mourning," she said, "like a group of women in black veils, wailing over the dead. Who knows?"

Annie had been doing a D.Phil. about the island of Giudecca and its mosaics when she'd met Harold. Her kitchen leaked in several places, and she'd placed a notice over the entry: Venice in Peril! Donations Gratefully Accepted.

It was at Annie's Easter egg hunt that I met Jessie, a graduate student from Columbia, visiting England on her spring break. She was working on F. Scott Fitzgerald, she told me, writing a paper on "The Unattainable (Unreachable) Female in *The Great Gatsby*, or Daisy Is to Day's Eye as Estella Is to Star," which title contained the cleverness the ilk courted. Annie included.

Jessie is talking to me about the eyes on the sign over the ash heap–bounded road by Wilson's gas station. "Obviously," she says, "God's eyes. Unlidded, unshut, overseeing the dreariest place on earth, and Myrtle's death."

"Poor Myrtle," I say—talk about a woman who has come to grief.

"Oh, it's such a fucking setup," Jessie says. "Daisy, Myrtle, Jordan. Goddess, whore, dyke. One's a sleepwalker, the other has *victim* stamped on her forehead, along with the tire marks on her ass, and the third cheats at golf, undermining a noble pastime—remember the suffragists burning *Votes for Women* into the greens with acid? God bless the male imagination, if there is such a thing. Linnaean to the core."

Poor Fitzgerald, he was in for it.

Suddenly, Annie's two girls, Harriet, six, and Susannah, four, are in the kitchen with baskets of red and gold and blue foil–wrapped chocolate eggs.

"Oh, please, please, please."

We agree to help them hide the eggs in the wilds of the garden.

The garden is bounded by a brick wall about ten feet high, in the middle of which a satyr's mouth dribbles water.

"Hurry," the girls tell us, "the others will be here quite soon. Mummy says she's about to go mad."

"The fourth category," Jessie comments, relentless. "Daisy in the sequel; Zelda after all."

"Okay, let's go." I take Susannah's hand, which she gives me eagerly. So eagerly it moves me.

Counter to the theme of wildness, there is a glass box set into the earth in a corner of the garden.

"What's that?" I ask, pointing to it.

"That's Mummy's special flower," Harriet says. "We mustn't touch it."

"It's quite rare," Susannah says.

"What kind of flower?" Jessie asks.

"Look for yourself," Harriet says. "Just don't touch."

Ganja in a cold frame? I wonder. But no. In the middle of the glass box, set deep into the ground, are the feathered petals of a protea, pink and black and white. Something African, a plant that descends from a bird, in its own conservatory, as an English garden grows wild around it, ruinate.

We fit chocolate eggs into cracks in the brick wall, under leaves heaped on the ground, in the remnant of a nest on the low-lying branch of a lilac, desperate to be pruned.

"Ready, set, go!" We finish just in time as a stream of screaming pink-cheeked children descend into the garden.

"Drinks!" Annie bellows from the window of the drawing room.

The rush of breath into another's mouth, a kiss taking us both by surprise. We're standing in the butler's pantry against shelves of Marmite and digestive biscuits and tins of Twining's tea.

Jessie wants to go to Stonehenge. Will I go with her this

weekend? I fear goddess-rapture but set that aside. Michael is away. I am lonely. It might be fun. I almost convince myself.

We agree to meet at Victoria Station nearby the theater showing newsreels of World War II and the Coronation of ER II.

Jessie arrives just as I do, carrying a bag of books—she has a terror of being stranded with nothing to read, she tells me—and a bag of food.

An awkwardness settles between us. The abandon of the hunt, the wildness of the children, garden are gone, and we're left out in the open in this dingy station.

"I brought this to read on the train," Jessie says, holding *The Well of Loneliness.*

Have mercy, it's worse than I thought. Nothing worse than doctrinaire sex.

Behind us people with paper cups of milky tea and packets of Embassy cigarettes are filing into the newsreel theater.

"Look," I say.

"What? Is there something the matter?"

"I'm not . . . Nothing."

Michael had called that morning just before I left for the station.

"I'm glad I caught you. I wanted to let you know I won't be coming back anytime soon."

"Lots happening?"

"They're bulldozing children, understand?"

"Jesus."

" 'They can't kill all of us,' " one kid said to me. "Another one asked, 'Have you come to frighten us?' You do understand what I'm talking about?"

"Yes. I do. Please stay in touch."

Just then the line cut off and I couldn't get it back.

"Look," I say to Jessie in the dinge of Victoria, "this just isn't a very good time."

I am in the British Museum, browsing, still in search of a subject.

There is a woman with a bag of cut-up oranges on the desk in front of her. She takes the oranges out of the bag and lines them up under the reading lamp, juice side up, on the slender shelf meant for books.

She wears a gray plastic raincoat; in all she resembles the day outside.

A blue-jacketed worker with a stack of books balanced between his arms and his chin says, "Madam, we do not allow food in the reading room."

"Oh," she says, "I'm not eating them. I'm squeezing them into the books."

Later, I will tell this story more than once. At dinner parties, a fine example of British eccentricity. I'll tell Michael on one of his phone calls, and he might be amused; he might say, "How can you bear that place?"

I will tell on this woman, in my small way avenging the sugarworks, the guinea-grass pastures, the blood-shot men.

She will become my stand-in for cruelty.

But something else is there. Something I resist.

Woolf's woman outside the British Museum, drunken, crying without over street noise, "Let me in! Let me in!"

Jacob snug in his rooms.

Is she not?

The cook at the institute, a large-breasted woman from Lancashire, set bowls of herbs on the surfaces around the kitchen, a minute space, fit only for brewing tea and making thin sandwiches.

She posted a warning on the door:

ANY FEMALE ENTERING THIS KITCHEN IS IN DANGER
BY ORDER OF MRS. AYRES

She told us that if we bothered her we'd become pregnant. She'd set the spells in place. She'd had it with requests for more hot water, she said, for more Earl bloody Grey.

Hadn't she got her own daughter with child when she wouldn't mind her?

Bloody hell.

"Bloody hell, they were burning the likes of me when all those pictures you're studying were being made. Burning us and our cats, and that's why they had the bloody plague, isn't it? Can't kill rats and their plaguey selves without cats. Once you upset the balance of nature there's hell to pay.

"My gran could turn herself into a crow and a fox. I saw it more than once. So unless you want to carry the child of my familiar, keep out of my kitchen. And tell the boys I'm watching them as well."

In New Zealand, years later, I meet another art historian who has at least one cannibal in her family tree. My claim to anthropophagic ancestry is the (perhaps) Carib hook of my great-grandmother's nose. No matter how blue her eyes, and they are as blue and deepening as the water beyond the jagged, alive reef.

I like to believe I stem from savages.

So does the woman in front of me.

When I smile into the glass of the museum vitrine, behind

which some of her ancestors are displayed, I imagine my teeth filed to sharp points, to incise the neck of an enemy, the throat of a lover.

She says to me, "Devouring one's enemy is one thing, but I've found testimony regarding the particular sweetness of three-year-old flesh."

We laugh as only women with cannibalism in their veins can.

She takes me to her ancestors' war canoe, also on display in the museum. I start to laugh. I tell her about crossing the Atlantic in a lifeboat.

"Are you to be forever a Caribbean Candide?" Michael asks me.

"Do you mean all for the worst in the worst of all possible worlds?"

We had a few more telephone calls, a few postcards flew back and forth. And then he wrote to say he wouldn't be back at all, and I could either stay in the apartment or I could leave.

The elephant man called and asked to speak to Michael.

When I told him where Michael was, he played the wise man to Michael's fool.

"Nothing but disappointment there, I'm afraid," he said, then asked me if I'd like to accompany him to the Great Rift Valley to tour the bones.

"No, thanks."

"You don't know what you're missing."

I decided to stay on a bit, on this island that seemed not like an island at all.

Later: WHO ACTUALLY DESIGNED THE NECKLACE? headlined an article illustrated by one of Michael's photos. A man's legs were bent back under him and his torso blazed, set afire by the flaming tire around his neck. Or it might have been a woman.

This is how I kept up with Michael, later—in the years after he left.

JOHNNY, WHERE'S YOUR CHOICE? WHAT'S YOUR HURRY? an armored vehicle, the fair and armed hanging from its sides, trundled through a township's dirt streets in the state of emergency.

I finally wrote Michael in care of his photo agency.

"Rode a horse last night," he answered, "white as snow, down a powdery road."

· II ·

{6}

Night Nursery

Richard had been considered by those in charge of literature the most promising poet of his generation. All that had been a very long time ago.

A thin-skinned, blue-veined beauty when a boy (framed pictures were set on the surfaces around his cottage; as time passed and visitors said they'd not realized Richard had a son—Stranger things, etc.—the pictures were put away), he'd been the favorite of master and prefect at his public school. Even the master who beat boys silly while they gripped an edition of Rimbaud (translated by the master, privately printed), even he fell for Richard, devout anti-sodomite though he was. He wrote letters to the boy in French, sealed with a kiss.

"Pathetic old frump," Richard reminisced.

As Richard grew older, he achieved moderate success as a poet, while his days as *puer fatale* faded into memory.

"I hope all this does not shock you."

I was sitting in the office of a senior editor at a publishing house in London who'd called me with a freelance assignment. He was in the midst of describing Richard and his work to me.

I'd noticed the boy sailors on the docks in downtown Kingston, heard the gossip among the servants about a certain cousin who fled to Miami every now and again. He used to go to Havana; that was no longer possible.

"No, I don't think so."

Richard's poems were dark, the editor said, casting shadows in the hollows of his face when he'd read them aloud at the Poetry Society.

"A haunted fellow, all right," the editor said.

He explained further.

Richard, tall and blond and blue-eyed, traveled alone into the mountains of an island off the coast of Burma and discovered a village populated only by men and boys, missing limbs and fingers and toes and cocks and eyes, the casualties of a war unnoticed by the West.

"Can you imagine?" the editor asked rhetorically. "All that hacking each other to bits. God knows what they made of Richard, all pale and intact like Lord Jim."

Out of Richard's sojourn came a poem in seven parts, titled "The Lost Postcolonial World."

"He was one of the first to use that particular turn of phrase, *postcolonial* I mean. Here, have a look," the editor handed me a thin volume. On its jacket one of Goya's *Caprichos* was reproduced: "El sueño de la razón produce monstruos." Night-flying creatures, owls and bats, haunt the sleeping European. I got the joke.

I

Within the bounds of Empire
the teeth are the first to go.
When the bounds break,
all hell breaks loose.
Chaos reigns.
By the waters of Babylon

the bald queen weeps.
The black queen eats
her young and gay.
Things start, wake
shake, rattle and roll.
Bantus confuse
sugar and diamonds.
Havoc wakes
Victoria Falls
over.
The bald queen has loosed
her stays   strays
The map turns black
from red   bleeds
Africa posts flood warnings
India presents in breech
of contact
Lady Mountbatten mounts Nehru
The Caribbean is ever more at sea.
"Now who will mind us?"

"Interesting," I said, handing him back the book.

"We thought so, although the critics did not seem to agree. Pity."

As I would no doubt say again: I needed the money.

Richard returned from his island of mutilated Fridays and took up residence in a small cottage in Cornwall, near the sea. He had a small private income, so real work was not necessary.

His neighbor, the editor informed me, was also a writer, also published by his house.

"She's actually an American, queer in every way but sexually according to Richard. Still, she's one of our biggest moneymakers. Her work allows us to publish his. And he knows it."

The neighbor, he explained, wrote bodice-rippers, turning them out one after the other, in too much haste to leave anything to rise.

"We'd like you to take the train to Cornwall and deliver the edited manuscripts of their latest books. I'll furnish you with a list of editorial suggestions to review with them. And we'd especially like you to work with her. With your background, that is."

I was slightly taken aback.

"Sorry?"

"We'd very much like to expand the market. Right now her books sell in the U.S. and England; we'd like to venture into the Caribbean. Do you know the White Witch?"[1]

---

[1]Herbert G. de Lisser, *The White Witch of Rosehall,* 12th ed. (London: Ernest Benn, Ltd., 1978); first published 1929.

"'. . . The story was that she came to Jamaica from Haiti.'

'Haiti?' cried Robert; 'then she is French?'

'Probably French and negro,' suggested Burbridge; 'I hear there is a lot of mixture of blood in Haiti; she may have some. That might account for her witcheries!' . . .

'She may have had a voodoo priestess for a nurse when her parents took her to Haiti; it is quite likely. And Haiti, we all know, is the very stronghold of devilcraft in this part of the world'" (127, 129).

Flash forward, 2002: *Celebrated Living* (the American Airlines magazine for first/business class):

"Local lore has it that the ghost of a beautifully mesmerizing, yet wicked temptress roams the grounds of a historic plantation adjacent to the Ritz-Carlton Rose Hall (876-953-2800; www.ritzcarlton.com), Jamaica's sophisticated yet secluded beachfront hideaway magnificently situated between

I did indeed. Mulatto Valkyrie—all heaving bosom and cat-o'-nine-tails—my fictional lodestar, born of my island.

"Through cruel fate the Lady Blaze Pascal becomes indentured . . ."

"I don't follow."

"Oh, Lady Blaze is the protagonist, our heroine, as it were. Where was I? Yes, the Caribbean. Lady Blaze. Perhaps there's a spell put on her. A wicked overseer. The heroine must always be in peril. Talk it over. That should broaden the market." This was avarice on the publisher's part. The bodice-ripper had a more-than-healthy—if that's the word—following. Her public clamored for her—eager to see her, touch her, impatient for the next page-turner. More than grateful for the author of their dreams.

Such was their enthusiasm, the publisher told me, that the bodice-ripper was forced to hire a stand-in.

I'd never heard of such a thing.

"Extraordinary."

"It's been done before, my dear." He went on to name a hard-boiled author. "You could not imagine the actual specimen."

The bodice-ripper found, with Richard's help, a superannuated actress and put her on salary, dressing her in baby blues and pinks and canary yellows, encouraging her to recline on sofas drowned in English chintz, wear eyelashes that resembled winged insects, her eyelids shadowed to match her outfits.

---

white sand beaches and the lush verdant mountainside poised above. Aiming to capitalize on the legend of the 'White Witch,' the Ritz-Carlton's captivating new championship course shares both her sobriquet and her character, as contends White Witch Course designer Robert van Hagge, 'Like her namesake, the course is alluringly dangerous and unpredictable.' "

Her as-it-were reading public simply would not buy a duck-tailed, white-shirt-tailed, blue-jeaned American butch in tennis shoes (as the publisher described his best-selling author) as "the font of Lady Blaze Pascal, ripe tits held aloft by wire, not a *pensée* in her head"—a joke he'd used before.

The actress—whom "thank God no one remembered; her biggest role had been as wife of a Crusader in something called *The Sign of the Saracen,* thirty years ago"—stood in as Caroline Albright and held press conferences in the name of seduction, passion, peril, what she called the rituals of romance.

Trouble began when the actress began to believe the lie.

"She was eager for another stab at identity. She was never comfortable with her given name—Bertie Morgan—yes; that's right. Nor what came along with that name. She passed herself off as a woman, an actress. When time ran out on that, she was saved by Caroline Albright. Truth really is stranger than fiction, my dear.

"'Please call me Caro,' she began to tell her audiences, 'like Lady Caroline Lamb, the lover of Lord Byron,' she reminded them, 'who used to enclose her pubic hair in her love letters. *Quite* the girl.'

"Suffice to say we could not stand for that sort of thing. She was becoming more and more outrageous in her portrayal. We were forced to put an end to it."

Bertie was out. The public heard through a press release from the publisher that Caroline Albright had suffered a disfiguring injury while breaking in a new mount and would be spending the rest of her days in seclusion—in a house in Spain with no mirrors but lots of paper and several typewriters—not to worry.

The bodice-ripper agreed to this solution and went back to writing from the safety of Cornwall.

Bertie resumed her search for someone to become.

"Remember: the heroine must always be in peril."

Not this heroine, massa.

Richard's taste in boys ran to the inarticulate. He once fell for a ten-year-old on holiday with his father and mother in Majorca, a boy from the Midlands on a package tour, who only asked that Richard help him assemble a de Havilland fighter from the Battle of Britain.

On the day the family was to depart, the little boy threw a barrage of kisses in Richard's direction across other package tourists immersed in their eggs and bacon and milky tea, thank God, Richard said, oblivious.

He told this story one evening at dinner in his cottage, with myself and the bodice-ripper present.

"How do you maintain their interest?" the bodice-ripper asked.

"One becomes rather adept at assembling model planes," he said with a laugh.

I felt a chill.

"In the States you might have to play cowboys and Indians," the bodice-ripper said.

"Yes," he said. "I just might."

"What's been your most unusual sexual exchange?" she asked, and I was terrified she was talking to me. But no.

"I suppose having a calf suck me off," Richard responded.

"I read about a man who trapped a duck in a dresser drawer, neck first in a hotel in Mexico City, and had his way with her. Makes a change from cockfighting, I imagine."

"That old *canard.*"

They laughed, rehearsed.

. . .

"Not true that his most sensational sexual encounter was with a calf. No sirree," the bodice-ripper said, whispering as if we were conspirators.

Richard was in the kitchen getting dessert.

"Pardon?"

"He once did a rim job on his nanny. Claims she tasted like Bovril, or was it Marmite—isn't that something?"

"I imagine it is," I said, as coolly as I was able, only able to guess at what she said. Lifeboats aside, these were very strange waters indeed.

"What about the night nursery, Richard?" she asked when he came back into the dining room, carrying a plate of figs and a pitcher of clotted cream, thick and yellow.

"What about it?"

"Oh, never mind. You'd do well to remember your lies."

"I haven't a clue what you mean."

"I knew a woman once whose first memory was of being in the night nursery and hearing that the *Titanic* had sunk. 'I was about four,' she told me. 'I remember jumping up and down on the bed, crowing like Peter Pan—Hurrah! Hurrah!—nothing ever happened, you see.' Children adore disasters, I think."

"What a dreadful place, the night nursery," Richard said. "Right out of your *Body Snatchers.*"

"*Village of the Damned* is more like it," the bodice-ripper said, "all those blue-eyed monstrosities. Childhood does take place on another planet."

"Speaking of blue-eyed monstrosities," Richard said, "Bertie's materialized again."

"Really? And who is he now?"

"*She,* Caroline."

"Very well; who is she now?"

"Says she's found a domestic situation."

"Wife?"

"Servant; but she has high hopes."

"Too large a dose of Blaze Pascal, I'm afraid. That sort of thing only takes place in bad novels—like mine."

I thought of other examples but held my tongue. I had no desire to engage in conversation with these two. I only wanted to pass on the editorial suggestions I'd been sent to deliver and make my exit.

"She's harmless."

"Did you do time in a nursery?" the bodice-ripper turned to me.

She had a way of asking questions as if she were taking notes, or maybe my inbred fear of invasion, of letting *them* know too much about *us,* was taking hold.

"Yes," I said.

"And do you remember your nanny?" she pursued.

There was no way I would speak of Winona with these people.

"Wet nurse, actually."

"Black or white?" Richard was taking orders for coffee.

"Not now, Richard. A wet nurse? Truly? How amazing."

"Not really; amazing, I mean."

Sometimes the Western gaze on the Caribbean was useful.

"Where did they find such a creature? I mean, is it common practice in your part of the world?"

Richard shuddered. "Really, Caroline, it's not as if there are ads reading, 'Situation wanted. Have tits, will travel.'"

"How would you know?"

I wasn't lying, not exactly.

I did have a wet nurse, a goat named Magdalena, who was tied in front of our house at the edge of the Caribbean Sea.

Winona brought her from country when my mother's milk failed. For company Magdalena had Winona and me, some chickens who roosted among the mangroves, and a pair of hawksbill turtles, for whom our front yard had been a breeding ground and who stayed on.

There's a family photograph of me sucking the milk straight from one of her teats like a wolf-child. Romulus or Remus. She was light brown, hairy as her namesake in the wilderness, with a black ridge along her back, running into her tail. Her eyes were goat-gold. Her teat was rough against my tongue, and her milk was thin and tasted salt like the sea.

"What do you remember of the experience?" the bodice-ripper asked me.

"Not a thing," I said. "I seem to be one of those people who has amnesia about her childhood."

"Truly?" she asked, stroking her chin.

Of course the photograph had been staged, an imperial allusiveness to the unlettered tropics. Sent round as a postcard. Did I mention the she-goat was tied to a coconut palm, that I was naked, brown, the littlest savage tonguing her wildness, that there was a full moon lighting the sea, that Winona in her white uniform was standing just outside the frame, waiting?

"Now there's a whole new public, Caroline," Richard said. "The wet nurses of the Caribbean, surely as romantic and literate a lot as British housewives or Celtic eunuchs."

"What do you remember, Richard?"

"About being suckled? Really, Caroline, you are grotesque."

"About being small."

"That it was extremely inconvenient. That I could not wait for it to be over. And you?"

"My childhood was just what the doctor ordered."

"That I doubt, severely."

"Oh, believe me; it was."

"Where did you spend it?" I asked.

"At a church camp my folks ran near the Everglades."

"You've always struck me as somewhat reptilian."

"It was quite wonderful," she ignored his comment. "I was left all alone while they carried on with their revivals and full-immersion baptisms and—yes, Richard, snake handling. I'd disappear into the swamp. I had my own boat, made my own world. I spent days on those waters just drifting."

"Very *Creature of the Black Lagoon,* I'm sure," Richard said. "Very 'Nigger Jim' meets the 'Lady of Shalott.'"

"Watch your step, boy-fucker."

"Speaking of which, things are looking up. There's a chance of a French boy this summer."

"Rental?"

"Sort of."

"Better lay in copies of *Tintin* and *Asterix.*"

"Tin soldiers of the French Foreign Legion, I think. I must telephone Hamley's."

They went on like that for a while, and then I got up and gave each an envelope with editorial suggestions as I had been told.

I left them to themselves.

{7}

Rex and Queenie

Rex and Queenie thought their names better suited to a couple of dogs. And they were right.

But being who they were, they kept them. And named their dogs Frank and Beryl.

In the cinema they might have been played by Celia Johnson and Ralph Richardson.

The two were naturists (i.e., nudists), and Queenie was a druid. Each solstice and equinox found her in a blue robe dancing on a hill in Dulwich, once making the front page of the *Daily Telegraph*. In the privacy of their flat on Clapham Common they went completely naked, even with company.

Rex was an atheist. He had once been a surgeon. "Long enough to convince me God could not possibly exist"; he said nothing of why. After practicing medicine for some time he lost his hospital privileges. This circumstance was alluded to but never explained.

Rex came from the island of Jersey and kept a house there, large and stone, overlooking the Channel and the other islands.

He explained his origins with such flair that I doubted they were true. As it was he and Queenie were almost too eccentric to be British. She reminded me of the old colonial joke where the Englishwoman bends over to pick up something at the racetrack, and immediately she is saddled and mounted by a local jockey.

"What did you do, my dear?"

"What could I do? I came in third."

Rex claimed that his place of birth was the prison ship *HMS Success,* where his mother and father were inmates.

"Launched in British India in 1790, she served as a prison ship for over a hundred years. Quite the showplace. Blue and gold escutcheons from stem to stern. Solid Burmese teak. Extraordinary—the attention to beauty on a vessel like that. I mean, for what earthly reason?"

"Don't be idiotic, my dear; remember the Customs House in Liverpool? All those beautifully carved African heads? Anything lends itself to ornament," Queenie said.

"Right. Anyway, her sails were painted with what was known as the 'broad arrow,' significant of purpose, taking those 'sent into transportation' down under, to the bottom of the world."

Rex said his mother and father were child convicts, accompanying their convict mothers.

"A dreadful business, my dear," Queenie said. "One had stolen a square of linen, the other had killed her husband; Rex can never recall which is which."

"One was sentenced to ten years, the other the rest of her natural life. There was no place to leave the kiddies, so they went along. The children of convicted women often went along."

HMS Success stopped at the island to secure cream for the captain's table. "Fresh from the tits of the nearest Jersey cow."

The child convicts jumped ship.

"They'd not yet been clapped in irons, you see. Those were being forged to fit. But they had been branded in the palms of their hands with the broad arrow; everyone was. Bloody awful, really."

Why couldn't this be true? Why was I convinced he was making this all up?

Their sitting room in London was a small museum. They had traveled throughout the Empire—"When it meant something"—and the bits and pieces they had collected were displayed on shelves, alongside the legends they had composed about each one's provenance, and what each represented.

I wanted to get a closer look.

In the dark of the sitting room, with the curtains ("Blackout curtains," Rex explained, "from the War") drawn and a floor lamp shining the only light, the curiosities were undifferentiated.

The pair had never married. "No need for that," Queenie said.

Rex said he fell in love with her when she invited him to Christmas dinner and served him bacon and eggs. "Quite shamelessly."

I first encountered the two while passing an afternoon at the Tate Gallery. I was gazing at a quartet of Rothkos, about as far away from the lapis and gold of the institute I could get. Rex came up to me and broke into my thoughts, making some comment about the darkness of Rothko's work and what could a young thing like me find in it except an adolescent assurance of the darkness of human possibility.

I found him irritating but of a familiar type; Queenie the same.

I did not rise to his bait. I felt nothing I could articulate about Rothko's quartet and certainly not to these two if I did. As I remember it, I was alone with the paintings until Rex and Queenie appeared. The Rothkos hung in a small room, each on one stark wall. Each purple/black vivid against blank white. The room I recall is similar to the room in my dream about the Mistral, but there is no sand on the floor and I am alone.

And then Rex and Queenie appeared and broke into my thoughts. In loco parentis? Too facile. Still, I never thought our meeting was by chance.

Together they led me to the Turners. "Why bother with these when a few rooms away is the real thing?"

I made no objection, and we ended up in front of *A Disaster at Sea,* which given Rex's purported origins was not by chance.[1]

They insisted I take their number. And I did and called them after a few days. I honestly don't know why. They invited me to dinner at a restaurant on an alley in Battersea run by a Russian and "his assorted women," Rex said.

I told myself it was a free dinner and I was living hand to mouth and I admit to being intrigued by the type. Too many J. Arthur Rank films at the Carib perhaps.

[1]J. M. W. Turner, *A Disaster at Sea,* c. 1835 (?). Oil on canvas 171.4 × 220.3 cm. Tate Gallery. Bequeathed by the artist, 1856. Possibly based on the sinking of the women's prison ship *Amphitrite,* bound for New South Wales, which sank off Boulogne in 1833. The ship's captain left the women to the sea, saying he had contracted only to deliver them to Australia. This painting predates Turner's *The Slave Ship* by five years. In each work the foreground is dominated by figures in bondage helpless against the sea, which will soon swallow them. The individuals are suggested in Turneresque manner, oblique but there, their anguish captured by the painter. In each painting a storm rages in the background.

So I met them at the restaurant.

They'd found the restaurant quite by accident, Rex said, and "were intrigued," as Queenie put it. They were collectors—people, places, things.

The outside of the restaurant was painted a dark red, including the window panes. The door was heavy, black.

Inside the walls were covered with photographs and watery prints of the River Neva and the Hermitage and Kremlin. The tables had small bouquets of pink and lavender flowers, plastic, thinly coated with grime, and ashtrays advertising those hollow-filtered Russian cigarettes.

On one wall was a photograph of the Russian grand duchesses after their faces had been blown off by the Red Army and before their remains met with quicklime. Plump-looking girls in pretty lace dresses sitting in an undistinguished room, but for the bullet holes in the wall, their faces missing.

Rex was immediately embraced by the owner, whose lips brushed each cheek. We were shown to a table. When I sat down, my back was to the dead girls. I was facing a small replica of the embalmed Lenin, on a knickknack shelf against wallpaper showing nineteenth-century scenes of life in the countryside.

Rex ordered a bottle of vodka.

The owner's embrace seemed perfunctory, part of the décor. He was tall, plain, but for the tattoos he sported on the back of each hand. One, a hammer and sickle, the other, a double-headed eagle floating above a cross and crown. Something for everyone. Like the bisexuality I clung to, and Michael made fun of, connecting it with my general disability to commit.

I turned my head and looked at the Russian girls once

again. I had seen four murdered girls once before. In a 1963 newspaper on the headmistress's desk. I was being punished for I can't remember what and had been assigned to polish the surfaces in her office. There it was, on the blotter on her desk. The edges beginning to yellow. BOMBING IN SUNDAY SCHOOL. A world, worlds, away from these four other girls. The headmistress came into the office while I was reading the article.

"You said you plan to attend university in the States," she said. "Better prepare yourself. They'll never change."

The vodka arrived and Rex poured us each a portion into a frozen shot glass.

"We should have sent for them," Queenie said, noticing my interest in the photograph. "They were our bloody cousins, after all."

"Try the piroshki, my dear. They're marvelous," Rex suggested, while under the table he passed me an eight-by-ten glossy.

I glanced at the picture in my lap. An elegantly dressed woman was swallowing the penis of such proportions she might have been a fakir.

The image was ice-cold.

"Recognize her?"

"Hardly," I said, passing the picture back to him.

"Really, Rex," Queenie said, "put that thing away."

"The countess of . . ." and he named a member of the aristocracy.

"Well, she certainly has the mouth for it," Queenie said. "Don't mind him, my dear. He loves to play the fool. He's only trying to shock you."

"Nothing to fear from me, my dear. I'm completely flaccid, have been for the longest time."

I accepted their invitation to the island several weeks later.

Once there, Queenie took charge, leaving Rex to browse among his books, on a glassed-in verandah, a bottle of brandy and a silver box of Turkish cigarettes beside him.

I followed her into a neolithic tomb, through a passage underneath a hillock that we negotiated in pitch dark on hands and knees. The passage ended in a circular space, a clearing where the dead were buried. There were a few shards scattered around and the traces of a winged creature could be seen on one wall. Light came through a circle cut into the ceiling of the cave.

As we gallivanted across the island, Queenie educated me about its history. It was famous for its numbered, overcoated cows. The brave behavior of the island people during their Nazi occupation. Developing bramble leaf tea, et cetera.

All across the island were Nazi bunkers, thick-walled lookouts where German soldiers watched over the Channel. I entered one at Queenie's urging. It was swept clean. I don't know what I expected to find, but I found nothing. Not even graffiti. I looked through a rectangle of space; there was nothing visible but dark water. Outside the bunker the ubiquitous cows grazed on a hillside, their numbers visible through a slit in their overcoats.

We got back into Queenie's Austin and drove some more.

"Look at that," she instructed.

Into a hill at the side of the road the Nazis had carved a hospital out of rock. There was a huge red cross painted above its mouth.

"Did you and Rex know each other during the War?" I asked.

"Oh, yes; I spent it here with him."

"How was it for you?"

"Not terribly onerous, once you got the hang of it."

The library in the Jersey house was offbeat, like the library of a hotel I knew on the north coast of Jamaica, where the tastes of many, their leavings, distilled into one idiosyncratic whole.

This was the sort of hotel where the guests disdain the white sands, native vendors, tourist traps, and ask to be taken into the interior, off the beaten track. They may fancy themselves Conradian and unwind with Scotch, neat, on a verandah overlooking a spectrum of blue such as they have never seen. No planter's punch for them.

Guests such as these bring along their own reading matter.

The Scalpel of the Scotland Yard—I remember that one well—the illustrated memoirs of the chief coroner. Black-and-white photos of bodies in various stages of autopsy and the instruments used in their dismemberment. *Magdalenism: An Inquiry into Its Causes and Extent.* Tales of fallen women: "Death-Splash Heard from London Bridge." "The Friendless." "The Crushed Daisy." "The Wreck." "An Awfully Sudden Death." The collection ending with the question: "Wherefore this great social evil?"

The hotel I am remembering was owned by a great-aunt whose domain extended to a neighboring falls. She was my father's relation, and in her honor and in thanks for letting me stay there on school holidays he painted a series of portraits of the hotel—actually a former great-house—after Monet's Rouen Cathedral, trying to capture the house at different times of day, in different weathers and light. The house, now hotel, had been burned during the rebellion of

1831, the Baptist War, and one painting showed a damaged wing, fires dying and smoke rising against a background of Jamaica Talls, a coconut palm native to the island.

Rex's library had its share of medical texts as well as popular novels, but the bulk of the collection consisted of pornography, titles like (and believe me this is no joke)

> *The Memories of Dolly Morton: The Story of a Woman's Part in the Struggle to Free the Slaves. An Account of the Whippings, Rapes, and Violences That Preceded the Civil War in America with Curious Anthropological Observations of the Radical Diversities in the Conformation of the Female Bottom and the Way Different Women Endure Chastisement,*
> by one Hugues Rebell, 1899
>
> and
>
> *La Donna Deliquente: The Woman Who Masks Her Corruption through Her Beauty Forgetting the Blemish of Darwin's Ear in Which Convolutes of the Ear Shell Are Simplified: A Sign of the Atavistic Female with an Appendix "Le Noirceur de* Nana, *un Roman de Emile Zola,*
> by I forget whom.

On his verandah, stark naked, Rex would revel in these treasures.

And yet this heroine did not sense peril.

Meanwhile, back at the mouth of the Nazi hospital: "Let's go have a look round," Queenie said, entering under the red cross.

Like the bunker, it was empty, clean of detail.

"Rex worked here, during the War," Queenie said.

"Doing what?"

"During the occupation the Germans insisted all local doctors volunteer their services, except the Jews, of course."

"What did he do here?"

"I'm not sure."

"What was his medical specialty?" I asked and wondered again why he had stopped, or been stopped, practicing.

"Oh, a bit of everything. It was such a long time ago. He's so much the better out of it."

The space in which we stood was a whitewashed cavern with a flagstone floor.

"Why would the Germans need this place?"

"Ask me another."

"I mean, surely they commandeered the local facilities?"

"I expect so."

"Well, then why . . . ?"

"Let me show you the operating theater." She turned toward an opening cut further into the rock.

"Was Rex a surgeon?"

"He was keen on it."

"What actually did he do for the Nazis?"

We were entering another tunnel, this one we traversed standing upright, Queenie holding her cigarette lighter aloft. The tunnel ended in a dark cave.

She held the lighter between us.

"Are you a Jew?" Queenie asked me in the emptiness.

"Pardon?"

"Well, are you?"

"Why do you ask?"

"Rex doesn't like the Jews at all. I've never understood why exactly."

"And you?"

"I have no difficulty with anyone."

She'd mentioned Jewish doctors, so I asked her the question that begged to be spoken out loud.

"What happened to the Jews during the occupation?"

"I expect they made do. I mean some of them shut up shop, but they managed. They always do, of course."

"They weren't deported?"

"A few. None to speak of."

I have seen the blue tattoos twice:

Once: when a saleswoman at Saks Fifth Avenue was showing me a dark-brown Anne Klein suit and the white-cuffed sleeve of her black dress drew back.

Then: at the end of *The Garden of the Finzi-Continis* in a cinema in Bloomsbury near the institute. A woman sitting beside me repeating, "I should not have come. I should have known not to come. Why did I?" When the yellow light cast by the overgrown garden washed over us I saw the numbers on her forearm. I put my hand over them and whispered to this perfect stranger, "There's nothing to be afraid of." And she whispered back, "God could not care less."

Queenie and I left the hospital without speaking.

"I expect you want to go back to the house," she said, getting into the car.

"Yes; I do," I said, feeling strange, uneasy. The quaint, the eccentric vanished.

At the house I collected my things, called a taxi, took my leave as cleanly as possible.

"You are a most peculiar girl," Queenie said, "grimly astute."

{ 8 }

The Joy of Cooking

[The] heart, which is firm and rather dry,
is best prepared by slow cooking.

— Irma Rombauer

Serious chefs should know how to deal with organs.

I had thought Elizabeth the most serious of chefs until I had dinner in her home, and when she drew back the cover of a silver serving dish that had been in her family since the Glorious Revolution, the most amazing yet familiar stench ascended, and her husband, Buddy, a Kentuckian exile, drawled, "Smells like the Piccadilly Gents' to me, hon."

Elizabeth flushed to her red roots and snapped, "And just how much time *do* you spend down there?"

The *down there* was pointed; the diaries of Joe Orton had been recently published, and we'd all devoured the tales of men's rooms, down there where the Styx flowed freely. Where working men in donkey coats extended themselves generously.

That was a big part of the fascination, of course. The spectacle of men with filthy hands fucking one another. Their presence wafting upward through the grating as we strolled to Covent Garden, down the Strand to the Aldwych.

The exchange between Elizabeth and Buddy ordained the silence of the rest of us, as images of Orton's toilets and urinals danced in some heads, until Isabel, Elizabeth's twin, spoke up—as, I had noticed, was custom.

The cloud trembled.

"Now Buddy, do be kind. I'm sure Elizabeth followed the instructions most assiduously. Didn't you, my darling?"

Isabel was dressed in a quilted velvet doublet, the color of oxtails, which complemented her double's brocade evening dress, pale like tripe. Each garment suggested a castle keep, swordplay, fourth-rate portraits up and down a staircase, all with one physical feature in common.

Each woman had a stately homeliness about her, radiating from the assumption that beauty was a given, given the title attached to her name. Each a lady in her own right. But then there was the mirror, cracked or not, quicksilver worn away or not, also in the family for years.

Orlando at each end of existence, they seemed, the bifurcated female.

Years of self-abuse with an industrial-strength vibrator had distended Isabel's labia to such an extent that there was a swishing, flapping sound when she walked. Her very own Hottentot apron.

Imagine Isabel on display. Yikes. Cuvier's favorite.

Tonight, thank God, we were spared the flapping. The labia were quelled by velvet trousers the color of underdone artichokes.

"I did indeed, my angel," Elizabeth responded, "to a T."

"And whom did you consult?" Isabel asked, eyes watering.

"Mrs. Beeton, of course; whom else?"

"No Julia Child or Elizabeth David for our girl, oh no," Buddy said, attempting to wave the cloud from his stinging eyes.

"My dear Buddy, Mrs. Beeton is tried and true, tried and true." Isabel came between them once more.

"Tried and true, my ass."

"Apparently," Elizabeth said, raising an eyebrow in the direction of her sister. Weeping by now, as were we all. The acridity of the atmosphere was relentless. We resembled a pack of professional mourners.

"I had no idea you were such a cookery book aficionado, Buddy."

"Christ, why can't you people say cookbook like the rest of the world," by which he meant the United States.

"Because the fucking Queen does, did, whatever, like the goddamn Castilian lisp." Buddy answered his own question, then blew his nose into a family heirloom.

"How dare you!"

Back and forth they barked, as the miasma from the ancient silver server settled over us, scenting even our tears, taking refuge in us as it escaped its container like a mad genie until the stench of formic acid—straight out of *THEM!*—overcame the atmosphere and the dining table, carved with fantastic creatures, demons from the mind of a medieval magus, became our pismire.

The table—ancient, in the family for centuries (what wasn't?)—was host to a mound of kidneys at the center of it, a silent thing, like plutonium, with God-knows-what half-life.

It was obvious that this wasn't a table meant for dining, but for something else. Contacting the dead came to mind. I suppose all family heirlooms served that purpose. "This is the cut-glass vase your great-grandmother on your mother's side took with her when she ran away with your great-grandfather. Their marriage was a great scandal."

I was about ten or eleven when this bit of family legend was given me. I asked why the scandal and was told by my father in a hushed voice although we were the only two people in the drawing room, "He was a servant. Such things were unheard of. Naturally her family disapproved."

"Were they happy?" I asked in my romance-comics way.

"They loved each other very much. So much so she did not care about hurting her own people."

This was the great-grandmother I never met; she died before I was born. I did not remember this great-grandfather, although I understand he was alive when I was born and I was taken to country to meet him. The only thing I know of this great-grandmother is her name, Rachel, and I keep the cut-glass vase in a safe place. Touching her presence in the crevices.

"Surely, angel," Isabel spoke to Elizabeth, "Mrs. Beeton advises on how to clean kidneys? Perhaps you neglected a step." She pulled a silk kerchief from the sleeve of her doublet and breathed into it, her sister's courtier staving off the stink of the court.

"I did my [*bloody* went unspoken] best, darling. What more can I do?"

Our eyes watered and burned, as if engaging her humiliation.

For some reason no one made a move to cover Elizabeth's shame. Good table manners? Taking one's cue from the hostess? Besides, who knows what might happen?

Elizabeth drew up slowly from her place, lifted the silver serving dish to her bosom, and turning, disappeared below stairs, trailing the all-but-visible fox fire.

It was her usual custom, someone mentioned, to vanish

at some point in the evening. Tonight the exit came sooner than expected.

Another guest opened a pack of Gauloises and we each lit up, trying to suck in as much smoke as possible, eager to inhale and exhale once more, while the sounds of weeping and the sweetness of Nepalese hash cut with opium (amazing, if unnervingly possessive) drifted upstairs. There was the crash of metal on the stone floor below us as the heirloom earned another dent, another evidence of family history.

The mist began to dissipate.

Buddy observed, as if necessary, that dinner was a total loss, and broke open a bottle of Remy, passing it around the table, treating it like port, Isabel said. No one cared to descend in pursuit of appropriate glassware, and so we drank the cognac unceremoniously, from white wine glasses and water tumblers, filling them almost to the brim.

One bottle followed another, until we ended with a decanter commemorating the coronation of Edward VIII—nonevent that it was.

Buddy raised his glass. "Fucking fascist that he was, and here's to his wife, the best cocksucker in Europe. Someone said being in bed with her was like being in bed with an old sailor."

Buddy worked as a freelance journalist; he knew all manner of trivia.

Isabel closed her eyes in disgust.

Elizabeth soon enough would be passed out, her head resting on the kitchen sink, her legs wrapped around the waste pipe for balance, the Aga on low for warmth.

"Well, Buddy," Isabel said, "another charmin' evenin'—'Nasty, brutish, and short.'"

But Buddy was well oiled by this time and ignored her Hobbesian assessment; he probably agreed.

We soon blundered into an incoherent discussion of politics and film.

It was difficult to get past the bizarrerie of the twins. Rumors about them abounded. I'd heard that they'd been lovers, and might be still. That rumor was mild compared to the rest.

Someone said that a strip of cartilage had joined them in the womb, tying them head to head. Supposedly if you rubbed their heads a nipple would tumefy where they'd been severed and they would tremble slightly. They'd been passed from favored guest to favored guest at their mother's afternoon teas.

What else?

Oh, yes. They'd begun as triplets but had killed the third child in utero—reducing her to nothing as they devoured her portion of placenta.

Whether any or part of this was true, who could say? But there was something uncanny about them. I couldn't figure it out, or Buddy's place in it, playing almost-eunuch outside their seraglio.

Did I really want a closer look?

Poor Buddy. At least a cliché, if not a type.

A blocked American expatriate (at best, regional) novelist, for the most part supported by his British aristocrat of a wife (his second wife; the first had been the college sweetheart, former cheerleader, who "turned queer," as Elizabeth told her dinner guests—"went nuts," Buddy corrected).

Poor Buddy, using the exhausted rationale of booze as a creative agent.

His imagination, he said, was all stopped up. When he tried to reach into it, images vanished as cave paintings vanished when faced with the smog of civilization.

"Ever see *Fellini Roma*?" Somewhat grandiose but that's how Buddy explained it.

We met doing freelance work for the BBC.

Oh, the life of a freelance. My last job had been for an American magazine, a research assignment that took me to the depths of the British Museum. Literally.

The London bureau chief of the magazine took me to lunch to a restaurant called Inigo Jones and described my assignment.

"You're not going to believe this, but there's a room in the basement of the British Museum that's known as the penis room."

"Really?" I responded with the requisite surprise.

"Yeah. Imagine. There's one little guy down there who's in charge of the whole thing. You know, wearing one of those blue jackets. It's his job to match the cocks with the statues. Some kind of civil servant, huh?"

"And you want . . . ?"

"And we want you to research a short article for us about it; New York will put it together. You could start with some background. You know, the Victorians lopping off the cocks in the first place, bloody hypocrites. See what you can get on Lord Elgin. But we want you to keep it light. We're going for laughs, you know. I'll bet most people who see these statues think the things fell off from age or something, wear and tear. No such thing."

Again: I needed the money badly; they paid extremely well.

I set out the next morning for the British Museum. With

a temporary press pass secured from the magazine I gained entry. Underneath the Rosetta Stone I descended to the workrooms. There were doors to the right and left on a long corridor. Did those chambers harbor other bits of humanity?

Breasts?

I finally found it. The card on the door had a name, followed by

MEMBER RESTORATION

The man in the penis room opened the door a crack and asked me what it was I wanted. I gave him the name of the magazine and he brightened.

I explained that I'd been sent to interview him about his job, and that the magazine would of course not treat his work as sensational in any way.

He said he read the magazine whenever he could get a copy; he'd read it since the War when he was a boy and was very pleased indeed with its obvious regard for Churchill, who had been his hero. "Everyone's hero actually, except for a few people—ingrates, really."

Could he get a subscription in exchange for talking to me?

But of course.

He let me in and offered me a chair. Through one wall came the sound of stitching. Someone mending the Domesday Book, he explained.

"Sound travels down here, all right," he said.

I looked around. There they were. Numbered in black paint.

The table where he worked—trying to figure out who went with whom, which was Hellenic, Hellenistic, Sumerian, Egyptian, Hittite, Roman, Byzantine—was in the middle of the room. All around him were his "chaps," as he called them. He held out the chap he was working on.

"This here's a particularly interesting chap," he said, "though one mustn't play favorites."

"How so?" I took out my notebook.

He propped the chap, carved from a dark stone—I'd guess obsidian—against the electric kettle on the worktable.

"See how graceful he is? Note the way the foreskin curls. Sumerian, I think. But whose? That's the question. A god? Or simply a lucky man?"

"How long have you been working on this?"

"Going on twenty years now."

"Don't you get lonely down here?"

"No time for that. The chaps are counting on me."

"Tell me something?"

"Yes, miss?"

"Was it official policy to castrate the statues? I mean, is it written down somewhere? Or part of common law? Or was it the decision of some overzealous Lord Elgin taking matters into his own hands, as it were?"

"Couldn't say, I'm sure. But we don't like that term down here, do we."

"I beg your pardon, but you must admit it's a bit of an outrage."

"What's that?"

"To seize something perceived as a work of art, to perceive oneself as the conservator of beauty, and then to mutilate it."

"Well, they were the Victorians, weren't they."

"And then to keep what they had hacked off."

"In case there was a change of heart, I expect."

"I suppose we're fortunate they didn't take black paint to Bronzino or Titian."

"I don't think it's in our place to judge."

"Did this extend to animals? Or was it only humans?"

"Humans, miss."

"And did they remove other parts?"

"Other parts?" Was there any other? he seemed to ask.

"Breasts, for example."

He reddened. "Couldn't tell you, miss. Not my arena of expertise, is it. Got my hands full with my chaps."

The magazine ran a small piece under the unfortunate headline "Penis Anyone?"—I got paid and the bureau chief recommended me to the BBC.

They were preparing a documentary about "Red Indians," as they call Native Americans, and had hired Buddy to write the script and me to do the picture research. That's how we met.

I combed the various archives for likenesses. From Her Majesty's Office of Printing and Stationery to the Royal Mint. The V & A where I'd researched the bell sleeve the year before for *Harper's Bazaar.* Imperial War Museum—formerly Bedlam. "Isn't that perfect?" Buddy said. Natural History with its taxidermied empire: savagely colored parrots, macaws, quits, frigates—side by side in oaken dressers. Dead almost everything. But no Indians, none apparent.

This was no easy task. Had I been in search of Masai or Aborigine or Zulu—Chatham Islanders, Maori, or Tongans—life would have been a lot easier.

I pressed on.

I finally managed to locate a depiction of Lord Jeffrey Amherst presenting blankets to the natives of western Massachusetts (smallpox virus not apparent). I found this image in, of all places, the China Manufacturers' Association Visitor's Center. It was baked on the center of a dinner plate. The guide said a service for several hundred had been shipped to Amherst's eponymous college. Along the rim, redskins raised their tomahawks against the muskets of redcoats. Until the dinner plate shattered.

This find, along with John White's watercolors of Roanoke (which I'd learned of in the BM Reading Room)—"Done to death," the BBC producer said—was the best I could do, unless you counted Pocahontas.

She was "our Pocahontas," everywhere. On the panels of a hand-painted fan in a flea market. Bare-breasted in the chapel of a TB sanatorium. Figurehead at Greenwich. Guardian of a tobacconist appointed to Her Majesty. Savage in fancy dress, dark skin set off by a crisp Beefeater collar, scarification concealed.

For his part Buddy drank the days away in the office the BBC loaned him. He finally took a kill fee for a dreadful piece of writing he tried to pass off as authentic Indian, excusing his awful prose by saying he was part Cherokee.

"I should be ashamed of myself," he said.

Buddy rented a room on the South Bank where he arrived each morning around ten, got drunk, passed out, had a late pub lunch or no lunch at all, and started in all over again.

He told Elizabeth he was writing his novel.

"What she doesn't know can't hurt her," he said, although long past caring whether anything hurt her at all.

He asked me to visit him in his room.

"I owe you," he said, "for getting us fired."

He poured us each two fingers of scotch.

He told me he wanted to write the real story of his boyhood in the Kentucky hills. His father's still. His mother's fury. His wars with his brothers in the back of a pickup. His sister. The glass panel between them and his father and mother and the family carbine.

Anarchy raged in the truck bed unnoticed, or if noticed, unchecked.

Each time he tried to start he stopped himself. Everything was tangled, ran together, shamed him. Everything was the bloody same.

His mother's fury was commonplace, like the anger of every other woman he'd ever known.

A matte postcard of a Main Street in a small American town. "Ye gods."

It was on Main Street that she took her fix every afternoon. At the fountain of the pharmacy alongside the other women forbidden liquor. Dope with ammonia.

"What?"

"Coca-Cola with a vial of smelling salts broken into it. A few of those and she'd come home roaring, 'Get your own damn supper.' "

His father's still, hokey and homemade, another American snapshot. Men dispensing liquor and acquiescing to sin behind a dilapidated barn.

"Thank God for sin."

Was he able to imagine what he'd heard? he asked me.

Seen?

His sister's gaze behind the shelf of scrubbed-clean Mason jars, waiting to be filled with moonshine and sneaky pete. The opacity of her eyes.

Could he have made it up?

Surely he'd be punished if he wrote it.

The moonshine heat.

A face in moonlight coming through the cracks in the barn board.

"I don't want to turn this into some hillbilly *Long Day's Journey*."

He said he couldn't see through the fog.

"Is that normal?"

"Common anyway."

The explosions of Saturday nights offered up for divine forgiveness on Sunday mornings.

Perfection was out of the question.

Sin was a wonderful thing.

How else to explain fucking your own daughter on Saturday night? When your wife was poorly and stretched beyond all hope of pleasure.

"Who the fuck do I think I'm kidding?"

Even when he tried to write the landscape, bereft of people, paint it against the screen of his memory, it came out flat, with all the conviction of Technicolor. Maureen O'Hara's purple lips kissing the Spanish Main. No shading. No place to go.

He came back to his sister, drawing an ellipse for me.

"What happened to her?" I asked.

"Nothing," he said.

His descriptions reminded him of the pictures on the calendars small-town banks handed to depositors at the turn of the year. Leaping trout, white-spired church, ribbon of telephone poles threading a country road.

Buddy took me upstairs one night not long after the night of the kidneys. I think we'd had liver. Elizabeth was rich; she went for the cheapest cut. She said she needed the blood, and organ meat and bones were the best source. She could suck marrow alongside any savage.

He took me upstairs to the marital bed, an ornate mess of curtains, draped around a huge four-poster covered with a needlepoint dandy and his greyhounds.

"Good bed to die in," Buddy said.

"That's romantic."

"No. Honest. This was the family deathbed at the old ancestral home. Isabel's idea of a wedding present."

"Have mercy."

Elizabeth was two floors beneath us, at her usual nocturnal station. Buddy and I undressed to the creaks and yawns of the old house. Drafts came at us through the windowpanes, under the door. My nipples responded to the cold, rather than anticipation, and I was suddenly shy. I pointed to a portrait hanging over the bureau.

"Ancestor?"

"Yes. Revolutionary tourist. You know, the kind who likes to wear fancy dress and fancies herself one of the masses. Supposedly she rode the barricades in 1848 and had herself painted in the act. Personally I think it was done in an artist's studio. Safe from the ordure of the mob."

He pulled me down beside him.

"I want you to see this first," he said, indicating a slender black line ringing his cock. A tendril, he said, stretching back to his mother, who tied a string around him when he wet the bed night after night.

I didn't know what to say, what to believe, so I just bent over and touched it with my mouth, and then Elizabeth was at the door, blazing, roaring with her head thrown back, like a scene drawn by the bodice-ripper.

"Christ! You really are the limit!"

I said nothing. Buddy said nothing. We shivered like children.

"What absolute bullshit! And you're a bloody fool if you fall for his tales of woe." And she turned around and was gone.

Down to the cellar—a subterranean Bertha Rochester.

But I was the Jamaican.

A few weeks passed and then Elizabeth called—the last thing I expected—inviting me to attend their son's games day. We were to start for the school right after breakfast. All was apparently forgiven; at least I hoped as much. Actually there was nothing that carnal to forgive, but who knew what Buddy had laid claim to.

Breakfast was to be women only. I was there, as well as Isabel, a female couple I didn't know, and Elizabeth of course.

The couple turned out to be a famous sculptor—a dead-eyed woman with a flawless string of pearls around her neck—and her unknown sister, bull-necked with teardrop ruby earrings. In each woman her attempt at femininity collided with a neutral, unsexed state. The sister looked like a farm animal—albeit one who chain-smoked, stubbing out her Silk Cuts in her heavy tweed skirt.

Another sister, Elizabeth whispered to me in the kitchen, had cut her own throat in the famous sculptor's bedroom, causing a terrible scandal a few years before.

"What happened?" I asked.

"A rather intense disagreement," she responded.

"Do you have sisters?" the unknown one asked me when we were seated at the magus's table.

I told her I was an only child, my mother having died when I was a girl.

"Pity," she said.

"Yes," Isabel said, "too bad you weren't two for the price of one, like Elizabeth and me."

"Do I hear three?" the famous sculptor asked.

And it occurred to me that one of the rumors floating in the amniotic fluid had come up for air.

"Let's not raise the specter of departed siblings here and now," Isabel warned, rising to fetch a silver ashtray from the sideboard in a vain attempt to save the tweed. She was wearing a long corduroy skirt, and even across the short distance her labia announced themselves in a faint applause.

What a way to go through life—that is, if she noticed.

"Pity," the unknown one repeated. "Had you a sister, we could welcome you into our club."

"Club?"

"Nothing serious, no oaths or anything, no drawing blood. Just jolly good fun."

Isabel was back at her place, sucking on a Player's, elaborately tapping her cigarette end on the silver lip of the ashtray.

The famous sculptor was staring into her sweetbreads.

Elizabeth offered coffee all around and said, for no apparent reason, "I feel so inadequate."

No one responded, and the famous sculptor turned to me and began to explain the rules of the game.

"We have formed what we call the Jane and Cassandra Club."

"Oh?" I said.

"Yes. After the novelist and her sister, that is."

"Indeed," the unknown sister said, "one thinks of the Brontës as, well, all tucked together on those interminable damp nights."

"Time to fly," Elizabeth said.

And they all got up as one. I begged off.

· III ·

{9}

Runagate

You'll have to take my word that some of these things happened.

Back at the institute a woman in her midtwenties came in cold off the street and was met by the administrator, a woman in her midfifties, with a slightly accented voice—she'd been born in the south of France. She'd come to London in 1944.

Above the two women, on the lintel over the marble entryway, was the word *Mnemosyne,* Memory, mother of the Muses.

She replied that her name was Catherine Lyle.

"Spelled like the manufacturer of Golden Syrup?"

"Yes," she responded, although she'd never heard of Golden Syrup and so was not at all sure.

She said she'd made her way through prep school and college on scholarships, chosen from among her classmates at Dunbar High School in Washington, D.C.

Her mother had been loath to send her up north to Massachusetts. Although she did not say this to her interrogator.

A girl began to sleepwalk. Catherine woke to see the girl rise from her bed—like *Blacula,* Catherine told me with a smile—and head out the door, down the stone corridor heavy with the dreams and nightmares of other sleeping girls.

Catherine observed this over the course of several nights.

Finally, she followed the girl into the icy New England

night. Outside, the two crossed the quad and Catherine saw they were headed for the school chapel. They walked up a granite staircase one after the other and entered the oak-paneled chapel with its huge likeness of the school's founder hanging where Jesus might be. The founder, a man of the early eighteenth century, remembered for his ecstasies amid the general drabness of Puritans. He had traveled beyond Pittsfield to preach to the Indians and turned the recalcitrant into bats. They might be seen at summer twilight, black clouds out of dark haylofts.

He returned from his errand to found this school among others.

The light over the portrait was the only light in the chapel.

Catherine stood by the entrance.

The sleepwalker made her way to one of the pews, crawled under it, still unawake, her cheekbones flat against flagstone.

Catherine stayed a while, watching her classmate, until the chill became too much and the founder seemed about to speak, as if to remind her that she and the sleepwalker were the only two in their class, and fortunate at that.

The next day Catherine thought over what she had witnessed and went to the headmistress to ask for her help. It was a hard thing to do. Her mother had warned her about making herself conspicuous, except in excellence.

"Always present a moving target," her mother counseled her.

The headmistress told her she was not to concern herself, some girls simply weren't up to the task; they would never fit in.

"I think you are different," the headmistress said, "exceptional."

Night upon night the other girl walked in her sleep until

one night when a watchman found her body hanging from a steam pipe in the tunnel under the chapel, where it was said the school provided a stop on the Underground Railroad.

Irony of ironies!

The headmistress used this lagniappe of history in her message to all the girls, noting (or inventing) the fact that the corncobs underneath the hanging girl's feet had been left by runagate people. And she quoted Robert Hayden's poem.

The dailiness of school life lifted; there was a sense of something heavy in the air. Parents, the white ones, flocked to the school, offering dinners at the Deerfield Inn. The people of the black students, including the dead girl, stayed away.

Catherine's grandmother wrote her that black people did not commit suicide: "There must be more to the story." Catherine's grandmother would say the same thing years later about Jonestown. "Kool-Aid, my ass."

But no questions were asked. The girl's body was shipped home for burial.

From the Greek revival quarters where she lived in aseptic bliss with her life's companion, the headmistress wrote a proper letter of condolence to the girl's parents.

"You must realize," the headmistress told Catherine, having summoned her to her office, "you must realize that most of the girls in this school have encountered your people only as help. You must try to learn tolerance."

Catherine tried. One girl told her how she used to sit cross-legged underneath the ironing board—"It made me feel safe"—listening to the ironer breathe. "It made me feel protected."

Tolerance drew further back.

Catherine would not forget the death of the sleepwalker

and slipped the gaze of the founder of the school. The worst had already happened. What was there now to be afraid of? Not some old white eyes long dead.

The headmistress—who, as is traditional, taught Scripture—asked Catherine why she had absented herself from chapel.

"You should have done something," she managed to say, and the headmistress dropped the question.

Catherine matriculated to Bolton College, where she encountered another portrait, another founder. Narcissa Bolton, abolitionist, feminist, suffragette, hunger-striker, and, as the brass plate on her frame indicated, "friend of Harriet Tubman and Sara Winnemucca, who she nobly protected and helped."

Catherine Bowman, a.k.a. Catherine Lyle, unbeknownst to the administrator is a wanted woman.

The pursuit of Catherine Bowman, a.k.a. Catherine Lyle, dates back to riots in an American city a few years after she quit the fine arts program at Bolton College.

Sister, Hanging did the trick.

In the dinge of a tunnel over a carpet of corncobs nibbled at by rats a girl dangled in a white nightdress. Catherine painted her own face on the girl. It was the least she could do, she thought, for not speaking, for not asking, "What are you going through?"

She painted a group around the girl. An archangel sporting butterfly wings and boxing gloves. The Black Madonna. A Christ with the features of Jimi Hendrix. These three stood to one side of the central figure. To the other were several people in caps and gowns, a man and woman dressed for the first Thanksgiving, a spinster in a gray dress holding a slender volume on which Catherine had lettered *Poems* in gilt.

The painting was hung in a student show the end of Catherine's junior year. The trustees of Bolton College declared the painting disgraceful, and Catherine quit the school.

During the riots Catherine interfered with police doing their job.

She found herself in a whirlwind. As windows were smashed and people ran through the streets, the police descended with teargas and guns and fire hoses and riot gear. Helicopters dipped over backyards, floodlights searching.

Catherine tried to stop police from picking up every female, from the grandmother pushing the Magnavox console across the buckling pavement to the twelve-year-old, her arms filled with Swanson's frozen TV dinners defrosting in the heat.

Heat lightning lit the street.

Later—when she thought it over—she thought she'd gone crazy. But what choice was there?

Black Mariahs flocked to every emergency room in that part of the city where—age notwithstanding—each female brought in was given a D & C.

On the line.

Catherine was (later excerpted in the London papers following her apprehension) violent in her interference. Out of control. Perhaps on drugs. A deliveryman (married, father of four, communicant) for a chain five-and-dime lay dead.

The administrator would never guess this.

But then Catherine would not guess that underneath the white blouse detailed with a Belgian lace jabot worn by the woman in front of her was a tattoo on the left breast—the Cross of Lorraine. She'd been a member of cell Gloria, parent cell Etoile. For the most part she kept her past to herself. It amused her that so many French claimed this connection out loud. As every German claimed to have served on the Russian Front.

From underground Catherine painted her Washington D & C Series, shown by a gallery in SoHo. The *Village Voice* sent someone. Her paintings (and her rank as one of America's most wanted) began to draw attention.

Pieces like her *Cop Scraping Womb with Nightstick* (acrylic on wood, 3' × 5') were startling, but considered by some overdone, repetitive, distasteful.

"Is This Art?"

When interviewed from underground, Catherine Bowman, a.k.a. Catherine Lyle, her back to the camera, her dreads in silhouette, said: "The state of emergency does not allow for subtlety, nuance in depiction. Those of us painting from this interregnum [thank you, Gramsci] do not use metaphor, nor speak in code. We wish to explode reality, not to obscure it, certainly not to beautify it."

The *New York Times* in a roundup of black artists singled out Catherine's work: "Rather overdependent on the palette knife but with a raw energy, intriguing use of color."

A journal of women artists, borne aloft on the second wave, mad in pursuit of a female aesthetic, questioned Catherine's technique, seeking a link to other female forms (quilts, china painting), and wondered why there were not black cops among her marauders.

The FBI suggested the gallery owner take the paintings down.

Catherine fled, then surfaced like a snorkeler in North Africa, crossed the Mediterranean, landed at Gibraltar, and headed farther north.

The administrator, for her part, had exited France through the network of the Maquis—a price on her head.

"And what would you like from us, Miss Lyle?"

She told the administrator she was interested in auditing lectures at the institute, utilizing the library.

"I think that might be arranged," the administrator said, and extended her hand.

It was announced shortly after Catherine's arrival that there would be a lecture by Millicent Redwing, world famous West Indian scholar, doyenne of a tiny intelligentsia.

Catherine sat in the back of the lecture hall.

I sat across the aisle from her.

The title of Redwing's lecture: "The Apprehension of the Negro in Post-Enlightenment Art."

Catherine took notes in a small exercise book with cross-hatched pages. Later, after she had left the hall, leaving her book on her chair, I retrieved it. What follows are her notes from the lecture:

Redwing: Put out the light, and then put out the light

First slide—Moor presents parrot to lady—artist?

Moor kneels on marble steps, turbaned, ebony

—like Balthazar on Afro-Xmas cards.

Hands stretch out, toward her pinkness,

ringlets, overfull bodice, falling backward, away from Moor.

Parrot—resplendent—sits on Moor's hand, upraised.

Colors: scream

Then: Fernand Le Quesne, *Les Deux Perles,* n.d., present whereabouts unknown—we can only thank God.

Two women—black/white—white languishing, as is usual in this pairing—according Redwing.

Black nude sets off white, mother-of-pearl bed—

Pearl = clitoris—acc'ding Redwing.

My, my.

Black nude looks out to sea.

Middle distance: ship w/sails

rescue? capture?

Next—

Aristide Sartorio, Diana d'Efeso e gli schiavi

Venice Biennale, 1899

Redwing: "Diana of the hundred breasts which nourish men & their illusions"

spare me

Black Diana

Breasts hang from her like sandbags

Promethean Mammy?

What *is* the point please?

Jules something-something

La Porte du Sérail: Souvenir du Caire, 1876

Ecco, homeboys

laid out on Sultan's carpets

panther in foreground with bared fangs—

portent?

Huey & Bobby

or Black pussy

(dentata?)

one brother sucks on a waterpipe

these homeboys all be stoned

Redwing: "You will note the passivity accorded the
black male in many of these works. His virile aspect
is sometimes transposed to the black woman, or, as is
the case here, onto the panther. These guardians of the
seraglio (most probably eunuchs) (nuff said) even with
scimitars are disarmed."

One exception:

Othello beside Desdemona's Corpse

Chassériau, 1847, oil on wood

My grandmother: on *Othello* in Harlem— '20s

Du Bois in *Crisis:* please would the audiences not cheer
when the Moor (Robeson?) smothers

Desdemona—

Native Son

O. raises pillow

D. offers no resistance

Redwing: "Some critics have described this Des. in a
'postorgasmic swoon.'"

Kill me tomorrow!

Let me live tonight! (come?) Othello, hornmad.

Jean-Baptiste Carpeaux—

Pourquoi naitre esclave?

you tell me

terracotta bust 1868

face: fury   movement: black/brown breast chafing

against rope.

Redwing: "The rendering of the female slave is a subject unto itself, which we can only touch on here. Suffice to say that in the *oeuvre* we find altruistic as well as libidinous motives."

Miss Prim from the Carib rim

e.g., John Bell, *The Octoroon,* marble, Royal Academy

1868

marble: the lighter the skin the greater the shame

check out Iola Leroy

residue

red hot

octoroon

rhymes with?

hair: from head to genitalia

chain: wrist to wrist

head down

no resistance

R. fast-forwards: stack of chained nudes

demure. rigid. light. dark.

supplicant

compliant

for me, life definitely does not go on

they can't shoot everyone.

I keep score

Fanon

Hansberry

what the hell—throw in Dorothy Dandridge

and Bessie Smith

et alia

ad infinitum

and now for something completely different

Jules-Robert Auguste, *Les Amies,* watercolor heightened with gouache.

B. nude on top of w. nude

w. nude, vacant. hot pink nipples.

Redwing: "Here the black nude, female, stands in for the black nude, male. This image, black body on white body, is not lesbian. That pales beyond what is signified. The difference in color between the two figures signifies the gender polarity of heterosexual encounters, heightened when a black man couples with a white woman. Note the muscled torso of the black nude, contrasted with the pink flesh of the other female. The black man would not be allowed anywhere near this idyll, if idyll it represents. The European artist always conceives the black man isolate, uncoupled. For example, wrestling a beast, or guardian of a harem, or, on display, a lesson in anatomy being sketched in the artist's studio. Only rarely is this isolation rendered with humanity."

As in

Winslow Homer, *The Gulf Stream,* oil on canvas 1879

only sugar cane for company

on the horizon a waterspout shades of Turner's *Slave Ship, Typhoon Coming On* this is where I came in.

Degas

Miss LaLa at the Cirque Fernando, oil on canvas, 1879

R: "While the black woman may grace the bed of a white woman, she also has her share of isolate poses. Here is one taken to new heights."

woman shot from cannon

circus performer—this is a true story we are told

in painting she hangs from rope by her teeth

arms and legs in contrapposto

note degree of difficulty

[Cf. Lois Mailou Jones, *Meditation (Mob Victim),* 1944— She knew the sitter had witnessed a lynching. She asked him to pose as he remembered the victim doing. She'd originally painted a rope around his neck, then painted over it—not necessary.]

Billie Holiday in L.A. once, a white woman asked:

". . . why don't you sing that song you're famous for? You know, the one about the naked bodies swinging in the trees."

I crave amnesia sometimes

that was in the air

like tales of "Gloomy Sunday"

its adverse effect on the big daddies of Wall Street—

and Lena Horne crowning a man at a restaurant in Hollywood with a glass ashtray: "Here I am, you bastard! Here's the nigger you couldn't see."

Militant blackbird   why bother.

Here is where Catherine's notes come to an end. Dr. Redwing, herself descended from blackbirds, John Crow, Maroons, saw her take her leave.

"Was it something I said?"

Shortly after, Catherine Bowman, a.k.a. Lyle, was apprehended at Heathrow Airport, and her story came to light. The police questioned the administrator closely, trying to decide if she knowingly offered safe harbor to a fugitive. Her own credentials, her heroics were revealed, much to her chagrin.

{ 10 }

Confluence

I have kept Catherine's notes to this day, showing them to no one, not turning them over to the police when they came to the institute with their inquiries. Almost everyone said they had not know Catherine at all, some said that she kept to herself, was secretive, et cetera. I was pointed out as someone of Catherine's acquaintance, which I had been, albeit briefly.

"Are you saying that you didn't realize she was a fugitive?"

"Yes."

"Did you not know she is wanted for an act of murder?"

"I did not know."

"Did she tell you where she came from?"

"Only that she was American."

"And yourself?"

"I carry two passports. One is an American passport."

"Not born there?"

"No."

"Where then?"

"The Caribbean."

"Which one then?"

I realized he was asking the name of the island.

"Jamaica."

"Lots of troublemakers there, I hear."

"So do I."

"With that hair; like hers."

"Right."

"So you say she never confided in you?"

"That's what I say."

"How many conversations you reckon you had with her?"

"I don't know. Three or four, I imagine."

"Ever share a meal?"

"We had lunch once."

"And where was that?"

I responded with the acronym for the School of Oriental and African Studies.

"Did she have any friends there?"

"I don't know that she knew anyone there."

"Who was it suggested you eat there?"

"I did. It has the best food in the university."

"I expect it does."

"You should try it sometime."

"Did you observe her with anyone else?"

"No."

"Are you certain?"

"I think she just wanted to be let alone."

"She should have thought of that before she killed that poor chap."

"What will you do to her?"

"She'll be extradited, then tried in the States. What we want to know is if she made any contacts over here with her own ilk."

"I really wouldn't know."

"What did the two of you talk about?"

"Films. Paintings. Books. Not much else. Tennis. We went out to Wimbledon."

"How nice for you. Did she ever speak of the situation in Northern Ireland?"

"No; not that I recall."

"Mention anyone named Maura O'Connell?"

"Who is she?"

"Never you mind. Let's just say she's up to no good. Did your friend ever speak of the situation in South Africa?"

"No."

"Libya?"

"No."

"Vietnam?"

"No."

"Palestine?"

"No."

"Namibia?"

"No."

"Sudan?"

"No."

"Zimbabwe? Tanzania? Brazil?"

"No."

"Algeria?"

"No."

"Cuba?"

"No."

The parade of nations continued. Then: "Do you know many people in London?"

"Some, not many."

"How well?"

"Not very well."

"How long do you intend to stay here?"

"I couldn't say."

"Must be nice, that sort of freedom. Come and go as you please, eh?"

"Pardon?"

"Are you a member of any cult, sect, or otherwise subversive organization?"

"God, no."

Why would I tell him if I were?

"Do you know people in Brixton?"

"No; I don't."

I was staying at my great-aunt's hotel surrounded by water. The sea in front, the falls behind the converted great-house. The wooden jalousies were turned down against the heat of the day, and the ceiling fan in the bar slowly stirred the air. Crawford, the barman, was polishing glasses. All was apparently tranquil.

I was walking on the white glass sands, looking down. A piece of blue glass, sharpness smoothed by the action of the sea, lay at my feet. I picked it up. The word *nuit* was etched on it. I fingered the letters.

I put the piece of glass in my pocket.

She slipped a membrane and slid into the interior. She was on a street that stretched gray alongside the River Thames. It seemed to her the past had no color. But then she's been used to looking at paintings struck with red and blue and gold. And she'd spent a lot of time at the movies where the past was writ fifty feet high and garish in the extreme. Played by Errol Flynn, witness at her christening, again.

This was something else. She thought not a dream because she could touch the cold iron of a balustrade in front of a townhouse.

In front of me a woman was walking, her skirts brushing the cobblestone street. She was walking and muttering. Her head was down. A chill rain was falling. This is not a dream, I thought, as the cold and wet hit my face. I shivered. The rain was gaining strength. I thought I would follow the woman in front of me, who seemed not to know she was not alone.

She herself was an opportunistic nomad, the scientist's term (but which branch?) for an omnivorous traveler, rootless. She collects terms like these, with which she will try to define herself. Poor thing, she chips away trying to find the form in the stone. Haven't the past months proved this? The woman she was following seemed to have direction. The rain was becoming downpour and the fog was thickening. Suddenly the woman in front of her came to a stop.

We were at Battersea next to the river. I glanced up the street to see if I could find the Russian restaurant. Of course it wasn't there. The woman in front of me lifted her skirts and began to walk down the bank into the waters of the river. But there were thick marshes between the bank and the river flow, and she could not get very far.

All of a sudden she turned around. The rain shone on her face.

"Will you come with me as far as Putney Bridge? It is not possible here."

"Of course," I said.

"Wait a moment," she said. "I'll find a ferryman."

And soon she was back with a man who said his boat was moored about a hundred yards away. He asked for payment in advance, which she gave him. Above his protests she convinced him she would command the boat to and from Putney Bridge.

We got in. She sat at the tiller facing me and I took the oars.

The rain beat at us and the Thames was rough.

She wore a sort of top hat and a heavy dark cloak over her dress. Her boots and the hem of her clothes were muddy and bits of marsh clung to them.

"What do you mean to do?" I asked as if I knew her.

But she was intent on the horizon and gave no answer as I rowed us upriver.

After a while she spoke. "Where do you come from?" she asked me.

"I was born on an island in the Caribbean."

"Saint Domingue? Of course not; then we would be speaking French."

I knew the place as Haiti but said nothing.

"Why are you here?" she asked me.

"I really don't know."

"Killing time, I suppose."

"Something like that."

"I've been in Paris the past few years. Because of the Revolution. These are tremendously exciting times, and no less because of Saint Domingue. Do you know it?"

"No, I'm afraid not."

"You really should, you know. You should see it for yourself. To see what might happen. What might spread."

This must be a dream. But then I felt the blue glass of *nuit* in my jeans pocket, felt again the coldness of the rain against my face.

"Are you my mother?" I asked.

"Oh, no," she laughed. "You have no mother, save for language. Besides, I am far too young to mother you."

So she was.

"But everything is of a piece."

I could see that we were drawing close to the bridge.

"The women of Saint Domingue wear spirit levels on chains around their necks, signifying equality. The idea of seizing it for yourself, you see."

She had me wait in the boat when we got to the bridge. She began to cross the river, then mounted a railing and jumped, feet first, into the black waters. Her wet clothes, her boots, the weight of her pulled her down, and she sank out of sight.

I stood up and pulling off my turtleneck and slipping out of my jeans dove over the side of the boat. It was terrible and cold. I went under the black surface, down and down and down. The golden guinea slid off my neck and was carried out to sea.

It gave me heart when I found that mirages could be photographed, that they resulted from the bending of light and were imaginary only insofar as every real thing was imaginary.

The Fata Morgana was one of these, the work of the witch Morgan le Fay.

I wanted to find the island on the map that was not there.

So I followed her under the water.

And this time she was not rescued to die of childbed fever, her daughter releasing her from the stone.

This time we were greeted by the mermaids of the unfathomable deep, those responsible for language.

When I came to, I was washed ashore.

Apocalypso.

Born in Kingston, Jamaica, **Michelle Cliff** has lectured at many universities and was the Allan K. Smith Professor of English Language and Literature at Trinity College in Hartford, Connecticut. She is the author of *If I Could Write This in Fire* (Minnesota, 2008); *Everything Is Now: New and Collected Stories* (Minnesota, 2009); and the acclaimed novels *Abeng, No Telephone to Heaven,* and *Free Enterprise.* She lives in California.